TREASON AT THE POINT

Other Books by the Author of
TREASON AT THE POINT

CLARA BARTON OF THE RED CROSS

THE GAY POET: *The Story of Eugene Field*

HOOSIER CITY: *The Story of Indianapolis*

THE LITTLE GIANT: *The Story of Stephen A. Douglas and Abraham Lincoln*

O. HENRY: *The Story of William Sydney Porter*

JAMES WHITCOMB RILEY: *Hoosier Poet*

TREASON
AT THE POINT

BY J. C. NOLAN

ILLUSTRATED BY HENRY C. PITZ

Julian Messner, Inc.

NEW YORK

PUBLISHED BY JULIAN MESSNER, INC.
8 WEST 40TH STREET, NEW YORK CITY 18

COPYRIGHT, 1944, BY
J. C. NOLAN

PRINTED IN THE UNITED STATES OF AMERICA
BY MONTAUK BOOK MANUFACTURING CO., INC., NEW YORK

For
LIEUTENANT COLONEL ROBERT M. KRAFT, U. S. A.
with gratitude and affection

U. S. 619673

CONTENTS

1.	SOLDIERS CROSSING	13
2.	KIRBY MEETS A STRANGER	20
3.	BY CANDLELIGHT	26
4.	"I DO SOLEMNLY SWEAR—"	36
5.	EMMELINE'S VENTURE	44
6.	JOURNEY AND ARRIVAL	55
7.	JED MAKES A TOUR	66
8.	VISITOR TO ROBINSON'S HOUSE	72
9.	"THE CHAIN, SIR!"	80
10.	AN AMIABLE YOUNG GENTLEMAN	88
11.	KIRBY'S INSPIRATION	99
12.	STOWAWAY'S FLIGHT	107
13.	A LADY AND SOME LETTERS	115
14.	ARGUMENTS AND STRIFE	124
15.	JED RIDES TO PEEKSKILL	132
16.	AN EVENTFUL DAY—AND NIGHT	139
17.	CONFERENCE IN AN UPSTAIRS ROOM	148
18.	THUNDER IN THE HIGHLANDS	157
19.	FATEFUL MORNING	170
20.	"WHOM CAN WE TRUST NOW?"	178
21.	TRAITOR UNMASKED	185
22.	DARKNESS AND TENSION	192
23.	HOMEWARD-BOUND	200
24.	"A MOMENTARY PANG"	210
25.	GRANNY'S SURPRISE	217

ILLUSTRATIONS

. . . the General, erect, motionless as a statue on a pedestal	16
A woman emerged from the shadows of the threshold	31
Behind the house the mountains were dark and frowning	63
A procession of three figures straggled up the path	89
"Sometimes a soldier is with him and they have boxes"	111
They swarmed up, snatching at the bridle	162

TREASON AT THE POINT

I

SOLDIERS CROSSING

ALL DAY THE SOLDIERS HAD BEEN COMING OVER THE RIVER, leaping clear of decks as the flatboats nosed into the cove, wading the shallows to the shore and then, in straggling lines, climbing the slope toward the road.

And all day Kirby Drake had perched atop the boulder, his legs swinging free of the tall marsh grass, his gray eyes intent, watching.

At first Kirby had tried to count the men, the horses, the cannon—those squat mortars on their low carriages, the longer guns with polished barrels. But as the hours passed and the numbers increased, he was content merely to look.

Now it was evening, the summer sun sinking behind the promontory. On the Hudson's east bank troops were boarding the last ferry. When they had crossed, the entire army would again be on the march to a new encampment; and Kirby, with no excuse for further lingering, would have to go home, to supper and to bed.

He slid down from his boulder, and stretched. He was stiff and cramped, hungry, thirsty—and vaguely disappointed because, though the day had been entertaining, he still had missed the special sight he had promised himself. He had hoped for a glimpse of the General. Indeed, he had confidently expected that, and in imagination had rehearsed his description of the incident for Emmeline and Grandmother.

"Yes, he was there." (This was what Kirby had planned to say.) "I saw him. I was quite close enough to *touch* him."

And his imagination, running on, had conjured Emmeline's gasp of wonder and delight and Grandmother's reply:

"Dear, dear! The General? How is he? In his usual vigorous health, I trust?"

It was always so that Granny spoke of the great man, exactly as if she knew him, as if he were a personal friend of whom she was particularly fond.

Well, Kirby hadn't seen General Washington. He sighed —and then brightened. Even without that precious detail, he would have a lot to report . . .

"There were scores—no, hundreds—no, *thousands*. Infantry, cavalry, soldiers of every sort in different uniforms, though all very dirty and patched. They needed a shave and a good washing; their shoes were in shreds and their poor, tired feet stuck out through the torn leather. Oh, they've had a hard time, plenty of fighting and trouble. But they didn't seem discouraged. They were sweating and noisy and rough—and laughing and joking. They called out to me: 'Hey, boy! Hey! Got any victuals on you? Got a biscuit or a loaf o' bread? Got a chicken or a ham bone up your sleeve?' " . . .

Kirby shuddered a bit, remembering that query about the ham bone. Hearing it, he had thought instantly of Patience, shut up in the barn with her litter of young ones. What a nice morsel of juicy roast pork Patience would have made for some of these famishing warriors! Perhaps that would yet be her fate, unless—

"Patience and the babies must have a stouter pen," said Kirby to himself. "I must hide them."

He trudged up the incline and veered through the trees, seeking a short cut which would put him quickly out upon the homeward path. The grove was quiet, with dusk sifting in between the branches. Kirby walked softly—and halted. Before him, poised on a small rocky knoll, was the noble figure of a mounted horseman, and Kirby did not have to glance twice for recognition.

He was seeing the General! There could be no mistaking the proud, calm profile etched against the forest green, the posture of the sinewy body in the saddle, erect, motionless as a statue on a pedestal. The rider's cloak was black and gracefully flowing; blue silk sashes diagonally striped his buff-colored vest; blue trousers were tucked into burnished boots with spurs at their heels. Firm and straight above the wide brow was set a three-cornered black hat with, beneath it, at the nape of the neck, a queue of brown hair tied up with a black ribbon.

Instinctively Kirby snatched off his own hat and crept nearer. Perhaps he might have nerved himself to address the General. (He said afterward, to Emmeline and Granny, that he had a mind to!) But just then hoofs thudded on the turf and a second horseman appeared, this one stocky and swarthy-complexioned, with hair glossy as a raven's plumage and dark eyes flashing.

"Your Excellency!" The newcomer reined in so abruptly that his steed pranced and pawed, forefeet in midair. "How surprising to find you here!"

The General turned, and smiled cordially. "Well, Arnold! And I never thought to see you in this neighborhood."

"I've been with friends at Haverstraw, sir. Surely you're not alone?"

"Only for a moment. Lafayette and my other companions are at the dock yonder. Since dawn we've witnessed the crossing. A prodigious enterprise—but done without a single mishap. These men are veterans, Arnold."

... *the General, erect, motionless as a statue on a pedestal*

"And now you're going south to Tappan, sir?"

"To Tappan," Washington said.

There was a brief interval in which the snuffling and shifting of the horses were the only sounds. Then Arnold said, "Your Excellency, this is the thirty-first of July."

"It is, indeed. July 31, 1780."

"The summer will soon be over and autumn upon us. And I, sir, am eager to resume my interrupted career of service to the cause to which I have pledged every ounce of my energy and my life's blood." Arnold spoke rapidly, urgently. "Weeks ago I wrote you, begging for an assignment. You have not answered. Am I to suppose there is no place for me—or that you harbor ill will against me because of the affair at Philadelphia, the false accusations, the persecution, the court-martial?"

"To suppose that would be an injustice to both of us, wouldn't it?" Washington bent his head, looking quizzically down at Arnold, who was a little below him, on the level ground. "True, I remember the court-martial, which I did not deem a persecution; and the accusations—some of which were *not* false. I reprimanded you as lightly as I could, in the circumstances."

"My conduct, you said, was imprudent—"

"And improper. I could not have said less; I chose not to say more. But I bear no grudge, Arnold; and I remember also your gallantry at Saratoga, your brilliant record, your daring and valor. Therefore, I want you to command the left wing of the army in our next campaign."

"An active command—in the field?"

"Yes." Washington's voice was warm. "It is a position of honor, and you will have your former rank of general."

"I had thought—" Arnold's expression had altered; he frowned. "The wound, sir, which I received at Stillwater. My leg has not healed. Perhaps I shall be permanently crippled, limping. It is not, certainly, too much to suffer for the sake of my country; and yet—"

General Washington, too, had a different look. "You refuse the commission?"

"No, Your Excellency. No." Arnold hesitated. "But have I not been recommended for—something else?"

"You have. Several of your former colleagues have mentioned to me the advisability of your supervising these Highland forts."

"Well, sir?"

"I said to them that action was what Benedict Arnold would prefer. The offensive and not the defensive. Of course, if you do not, if there's some charm for you in being steward to our extensive stores and provisions along the Hudson, in overseeing the garrison at West Point—"

"Well, sir?" Arnold said again, and eagerly.

Before Washington could respond, a shout echoed from below and several officers mounted from the river's brink to the edge of the grove.

"It is my escort," said General Washington. "The shouting indicates that the ferrying has been completed. I shall go with Lafayette and his staff members to the tavern three miles downstream. Colonel Alexander Hamilton will be there. Will you not join us for supper, Arnold? We can then discuss this matter."

"No, I thank you, sir."

"You will be treated with utmost consideration. Bygones will be bygones."

Arnold ruefully shook his head. "But, sir, if I might talk with you tomorrow, at your convenience?"

"You may, indeed."

"And privately?"

"Yes. Come to Tappan in the morning."

Arnold bowed. "I shall wait upon you there. You must believe that I am grateful to you, sir."

"And you must believe that I am and always have been your friend." Spurring his horse, Washington descended from the knoll and for an instant laid his hand on Arnold's shoulder. "Until tomorrow, then?"

"Until tomorrow, Your Excellency."

As General Washington rode away, Arnold sat gazing after him. The brooding silence of evening flowed into the grove—and presently was disrupted by a sudden growl of thunder, a weird noise that came from a cloudless sky, breaking, swelling, subsiding. Arnold seemed to listen acutely but without alarm. He drew a handkerchief from his sleeve and wiped his swarthy countenance, and brushed back his glistening hair. The thunder rumbled again. He brought his whip down smartly upon the flank of the big chestnut mare; and with something grim and inscrutable in his attitude, he cantered off, threading a swift, perilous course through the trees.

2

KIRBY MEETS A STRANGER

WHEN THE HOOFBEATS WERE QUITE FAINT, KIRBY DRAKE pulled up from the bushes in which, by no particular wish of his own, he had been concealed. The thunder had not frightened him, for though some people in the Hudson Highlands believed it to be a mysterious omen of impending disaster, Kirby was not so superstitious. No, the thunder was only the result of a combination of atmospheric conditions, and it was harmless. Yet it did remind Kirby that night was falling, that he was really rather late and that perhaps Grandmother might be worrying about him.

He began to walk northward and to hurry.

He did not reproach himself for having loitered—to see General Washington was surely a rare reward!—and the conversation which he had overheard would make an interesting addition to the narrative he would soon be giving Granny and Emmeline. Kirby would never have known who General Arnold was, had the gentleman not been addressed by name; but now he recalled that earlier in the year Benedict Arnold had paid a visit to this region, touring and inspecting the fort at West Point and all the craggy garrisons surrounding it. Without comprehending the reference of both generals to "the affair in Philadelphia," Kirby felt that the subject might be intriguing. He would ask someone to tell him about it.

"I'll ask Granny," thought Kirby, who had more curiosity

than most boys of ten. "She will know. Granny knows simply *everything*."

It was now very dark except for the moon, a pale gold disc just peeping above the bluff. Kirby quickened his pace. The road was lonely, with no other pedestrians, not a soul, about. But then, when he was within a half-mile of home, Kirby became aware of footsteps behind him. They seemed to have had no definite starting—and no end, and they were in perfect rhythm with his own.

"Really," thought Kirby, after a while, "I liked being lonely better than I like the footsteps."

Where the road was overhung with trees and the bluffs frowned, eerie as a tunnel, Kirby glanced cautiously over his shoulder. He couldn't see anybody. Or *could* he? Was that a shape more substantial than shadow bobbing and ducking under the trailing boughs of the willow? He walked faster, and the footsteps were faster. He slowed; the footsteps were more leisurely.

"It's just my fancy," said Kirby to himself. "It must be—and I'll prove it!"

He stopped.

But the footsteps did not stop. They came on—and on; and a hand seized Kirby by the tail of his shirt.

"Why the haste, my lad?" demanded a deep voice.

Tottering, Kirby turned and confronted the owner of the footsteps and the voice. A soldier, a tall, gaunt person in cocked hat and tattered regimentals, a stranger.

"S—sir?" stammered Kirby. "S—sir?"

And then the tall, gaunt stranger laughed.

"Oh, Jed!" cried Kirby. "It's *you!*"

"Your brother. Yes, Kirby."

"You wanted to play a trick on me." Kirby fumbled for his brother's hand and clasped it. "You wanted to scare me."

"I did scare you."

"But why are you here?" Kirby had not seen Jed for months; he scarcely could realize that he was seeing him now. "Have you got a furlough? Were you with the troops at the ferry?"

"One question at a time, Bud." Jed linked Kirby's arm through his. "I *have* got a furlough; I'm here because I was granted a few days off to go home; but I wasn't with the men who crossed the river. I've been transferred; this week I've been with General Lafayette's men, or occasionally with Colonel Hamilton—I just do whatever I'm told to do. Yesterday I ferried with a squad sent to patrol the camp site at Tappan."

"You must be very important, Jed."

"No, very *unimportant*."

"I don't believe it!"

"Don't you?" Jed chuckled. "Oh, well, more of that when we are at the cottage and Granny and Emmeline have fed me. Come! Speed it up!"

Obediently and speedily Kirby pattered, and smiled in the darkness. "They'll be very happy, Jed."

"Yes, I think they will. How are they, anyway?"

"Both all right. I've been taking care of them."

"Certainly you have. I knew you would."

"But things have been bad since you left. There was the battle at Stony Point. The British captured it."

"That was in June of last year. Yes, and then Wayne recaptured it, eh?"

"In July," Kirby said. "Mad Anthony Wayne. Such fighting, Jed! Farms were destroyed all about, crops ruined, gardens trampled. The British burned Continental Village over the river."

"I heard about it," Jed said soberly. "But you weren't hurt?"

"Not ourselves, no. But you know how the cottage stands,

the west wall and chimney projecting almost into the road? Well, in the skirmishing a cannonball hit the wall and knocked it and the chimney into smithereens."

"For heaven's sake, Kirby!"

"Oh, it was very bad—though it might have been worse, if we'd been in the cottage. But we weren't. We'd gone up into the hills, where many people were hiding. We didn't know about the chimney until later, when we got back."

"Has the damage been repaired?"

"Well," Kirby said, "yes—and no."

"What's that mean?" Jed demanded.

"We did the best we could. We had the same old stones and we stacked them up and pasted them together with a plaster that Granny mixed. The wall looks quite good. And the chimney is only a *little* crooked. But it won't draw."

"The chimney won't draw?"

"Not much. All winter the house was full of smoke, and Granny got a cough. I suppose we'd have done better if we could have bought lime for the plaster."

"Haven't you any money, Kirby?"

"No. Have you?"

"None," Jed said gruffly. "None."

Kirby was consoling. "Oh, well. We've been very comfortable, really. This summer we cook outside, mostly. Granny doesn't cough now; and with the weather so fine, we don't need a good chimney."

"But you will," Jed said, "with winter coming on. Have you had food, Kirby?"

"Oh, yes! More than we could use—almost. I tend Granny's garden. It was spared; providentially, she says. And Granny sews for the Joshua Smiths and they pay her with flour—when they *have* flour. And Emmy's hens lay lots of eggs. We have sugar and salt. And what do you think, Jed? Patience has five little pigs!"

"Five? Patience is a noble porker."

"Isn't she? I love Patience!"

"Five pigs? You'll not starve, Kirby."

"But we wouldn't *eat* them! Why, that would be like eating our kinfolks!" Kirby thought a moment of the soldiers. No one must know about Patience's family!

Jed was stalking on. "She oughtn't to stay here," he said. "Not even if you get the chimney fixed—and you probably won't. There may be more fighting. The talk is that the British are bound to attack West Point, if ever they have the chance. Or they might try for Stony Point again. No, no! It's dangerous for her to stay here. She's so old—"

"Old? She isn't, at all! Patience is *young*. Just four."

"Not Patience, Kirby. *Granny*. Granny is old, and she ought to go to some safer place."

"To Uncle Tom in Rhode Island?"

"There," said Jed, "or somewhere."

"Traveling would cost money, though."

"Yes. I guess Emmeline hasn't any money, either?"

"Of course not! Where would she get it? Emmy once said that Granny ought to go to Uncle Tom's; but Granny said no, she wouldn't; she'd always lived in the cottage, since the day she was born and nobody could chase her out—and certainly not the British! She said she liked New York, and now she's at an age where *things* mean more to her than just her own safety."

"What things?" Jed asked.

"Oh, the garden, and the maples Grandfather planted by the shed forty-one years ago, in 1739. And the vines twining on the fence. Granny said Emmy is only a foolish child of fifteen and wouldn't understand."

"But I'm sixteen," Jed asserted. "Granny may not have

listened to Emmy, but she'll listen to me. Boys, Kirby, have more sense than girls."

"Yes," Kirby agreed. "Much more." He paused. "You think you can persuade Granny to go to Uncle Tom's?"

"I think so."

"Even when she has no money?"

"There it is, in a nutshell!" Jed said, and his young voice was harsh. "No money. We always bump into that. But I shall arrange for it, somehow. I've these few days to arrange it. I'll concentrate, and—I'll do it!"

Kirby skipped blithely. He had not been so much concerned with Granny's plight; but he was positive that if a problem existed, Jed would solve it. Jed was wonderful, so big and brawny; under his coat sleeve, his muscles were hard as iron.

And just ahead was the cottage, a candle showing its yellow gleam through the window; the silhouette of eaves sketched as if in ink against the night sky. Granny and Emmeline must surely be stirring kettles and porringers.

"Hi-yi!" sang Kirby. "Supper! I can smell it, can't you, Jed?"

3

BY CANDLELIGHT

"I SAW GEORGE WASHINGTON," KIRBY SAID. "I DID! I WAS SO close I could have touched him. But I didn't."

"Dear, dear!" exclaimed Grandmother. "I hope he's bearing up. A good man, honest all through; and no frills or furbelows or language that says one thing and means another. We can depend on General Washington."

Kirby glowed. Everything was going just as he'd planned it. Nine o'clock, the dishes washed and put away, the Drakes assembled around the brace of flickering candles in the big kitchen—and Kirby himself the center of attention. Slim and silver-haired, Grandmother sat in her chair and smiled into Kirby's shining eyes. She smiled at Emmeline, whose smooth flaxen head was bent above her knitting. Perhaps Grandmother smiled oftenest and most tenderly at Jed, who had stretched himself to rest, full-length, on the pine floor. But this, Kirby felt, was only right, because Jed had been so long away.

Nothing, surely, could be pleasanter than their being all together again, an intimate circle. Outside the wind had risen, but it was only a south wind, murmuring and never whistling through the chinks in the faulty plaster. Grandmother had draped strips of cloth from the ceiling to hide the havoc of a cannonball. Swaying and billowing, the improvised curtain lent the room a cozy sort of charm.

Grandmother picked up from her lap the purplish-red silk on which she was sewing. "What would become of us if we didn't have George Washington? I really don't know, my dears! The country is honeycombed with spies. Or these so-called Loyalists—they're enemies too. In war, people are either for or against you, and no middle ground. Neutrality? It's so much bosh! I suppose it isn't practical to arrest all the Loyalists and lock them up—they're so many and scattered. But I would be in favor of it."

"Is Mr. Joshua Smith a Loyalist, Granny?" Kirby asked.

"No one has said so." Behind steel-rimmed spectacles, her eyes were anxious. "At least, not openly."

"But his brother is."

"Yes. Mr. Smith's brother is the Loyalist chief justice in New York. And this claret-colored silk is to be the stylish coat which Mistress Smith engaged me to stitch up for her husband."

"And Mr. Smith's a wealthy man—and *not* in the army."

"But all that doesn't prove anything, Kirby."

"Mr. Smith may be just too fat to be a soldier. He's awfully fat."

"Perhaps." Grandmother sighed.

"You wouldn't sew a stylish coat for an enemy, would you, Granny?"

"No, I wouldn't. Oh, I declare," Grandmother said, "one of the worst things about this war is that it makes you suspicious of everyone, even of your neighbors!" She jabbed a length of gold thread through her needle. "I do hate the war!"

"And King George," Kirby said. "Don't you hate King George, Granny?"

"Not so much, no."

"You *don't?*" Kirby was scandalized.

"He's probably no better than he should be, but it's not the king we're fighting."

"Oh, Granny, it *is!*"

"No." She measured the silk for a buttonhole. "It's what he stands for, Kirby. Ideas, traditions, beliefs. Whoever was on the throne of England now, the war would have to be fought. King George is just a symbol, and I can't find it in my heart to hate him."

"I can!" Kirby said.

"You're like most folks, Bud," said Jed lazily, from the floor. "A symbol won't do. You've got to have a person, a man, to be mad at, to see and blame for all the mischief."

"I blame King George," said Kirby.

"But Granny's right, just the same," Jed grinned. "Have you thought that Mr. Joshua Smith may be a secret agent? They say a lot of them are around, gathering information. It's rated as a valuable service. Not quite spying, but something like it. Take our Mr. Smith, for example. We don't know what he is, no one seems to know; and therefore he probably is allowed to roam wherever he pleases, behind the British lines, behind our lines—anywhere. Sometimes he's called a shirker or a traitor; he can't answer such charges, can never reveal his identity or what he is doing—"

Emmeline glanced up from her knitting; she was pink-cheeked and demure, her eyes as blue as violets. "That isn't fair, Jed. Mr. Smith isn't a secret agent; he may not even be a Loyalist."

"Oh, well, I was just supposing."

"Mr. Smith may be a patriot," said Emmeline.

"I think he is," said Grandmother. "Very probably."

"Then he ought to *say* what he is," said Kirby.

Emmeline spread her knitting over her knee. "If Mr. Smith were a Loyalist, General Arnold wouldn't be his friend, would he? And I heard in the village this afternoon that General Arnold is at the Smith house now. I also heard he's to be the new commandant at West Point."

"General Arnold at West Point?" Kirby, feeling im

portant, would have denied this. But he hadn't the chance. Suddenly, out in the road, was the sound of someone kicking and shuffling through the gravel and a voice upraised in a rollicking tune.

> " 'Yankee Doodle came to town,
> Riding on a pony,' " . . .

"Hark!" Jed sat up. "What's that, Emmy? Don't you heed it?"

"Certainly, I do. It's the new song. *Our* song."

"I know. But who's singing it at this hour o' the night? What *woman* would be out there in the dark—"

"It must be Captain Molly," Emmeline said, and as Jed looked bewildered, she went on: "Mistress Hays. Molly Pitcher, they call her in the village; she lives up near Buttermilk Falls."

"They call her Dirty Kate too, Jed," added Kirby, helpfully.

"Kirby!" Emmeline was shocked. "You naughty boy!"

"Well, they do. And they laugh at her."

"*You* musn't," Granny said, "or I'll punish you. Dirty Kate, indeed! For shame!"

The song was shriller every minute, and very gay.

> " 'Father and I went down to camp,
> Along with Captain Good'in,
> Where we see the men and boys
> As thick as hasty-*puddin'* . . .' "

"I expect," Kirby said, his head tilted, and listening, "that she's been tippling again—"

"Kirby, will you be *still?*" Emmeline cried. "I won't have you talking so! Molly Pitcher is a heroine. She was at Monmouth, and so brave that General Washington commissioned her as an army sergeant; and before that, she was at Fort Clinton; and now she's retired on half-pay pension—"

"And living at Buttermilk Falls?" Jed got to his feet. "Don't quarrel, children. I'm interested in this Captain Molly. Why don't you invite her in, Granny?"

"I will—and give her a cup of tea. But if you dare make fun of her, Kirby Drake—!"

"No, ma'am."

Grandmother shook a warning finger, and then stepped to the door. "Captain Molly! Oh, Captain Molly!"

The singing ceased and a woman emerged from the shadows of the threshold. She was young and robust, her red hair tumbled and untidy under a soldier's cocked hat. She wore a military jacket, buttoned above full, ruffled and somewhat bedraggled skirts. She balanced rather unsteadily in the door, but her smile was wide and merry.

"You were hailin' me, Mistress Drake?"

"Yes." Grandmother said. "This is my grandson, Jeremiah. He wants to meet you?"

"Does he, now?" Captain Molly looked pleased. "Another trooper, eh?"

Jed bowed. "With Washington, ma'am."

"God bless His Excellency!" Molly exclaimed piously. "I been down to the tavern all day, watchin' 'em go by." She accepted the stool which Jed placed for her. "Thank 'ee . . . Yes, sir, some were French troops, marchin' from t'other direction. Yelled at me, they did, and tossed pennies into me hat." She put up her hand to her hatbrim and there was the jingle of metal. "I yelled right back at the Frenchies. 'Don't you jeer at me,' I says, 'for I'm a good respectable girl, I am, and an officer, besides!' Ah, but they meant not a mite of harm, and I wasn't angry."

Grandmother was taking the tea pot from the hob, while Emmeline fetched a cup. When the cup was filled, Emmeline brought it to the guest.

"Thank 'ee kindly." Captain Molly sipped the tea. "Very

A woman emerged from the shadows of the threshold

good it is, Mistress Drake, and better *for* me than some of the things I've had to drink at the tavern, no doubt." She giggled and winked, and held her finger quirked out over the handle in a manner intended to be dainty. When she had emptied the cup, she wiped her lips on her jacket sleeve. "Mistress Drake, they tell me you're a seamstress?"

"I am," Grandmother said, "though I don't get much sewing to do these days."

"Ah, then you might have the time to make me some petticoats. I'd pay promptly—which is more'n many people can promise."

"Yes, I would have the time, Captain Molly."

"That's nice. And I'll buy the linen." Beaming complacently, she turned to Jed. "I'm rich, I am. Every month, reg'lar as clockwork, I draw me pension. Did you know I had a pension?"

"I heard about it," said Jed.

"Because of Fort Clinton. I fired the last shot there, before we surrendered to the British. They were scalin' the ramparts, the British were, and me husband—that's John Hays—dropped his match and fled from his gun. 'Come on, Molly!' he shouted. 'Well,' I thought, 'one more blast at the scoundrels'—so quick as scat, I caught up the match and touched off the powder. Then *I* scampered. And at Monmouth, all day I carried water to John and the others at the guns, and when poor John fainted dead away, from the heat, I saw his cannon idle and I said to meself, 'What I've done once, I can do again. There's no reason I shouldn't have John's station, for I'm as good as any man in the forces!'"

"So with that, you proved it," Emmeline said. "You were splendid, Captain Molly."

"Ah, no doubt, anyone else would have done as much dearie." But Molly was gratified at the praise, and her eyes brightened reminiscently. "The next morning after Monmouth, General Greene came and led me to General Washington, as he sat, very grand, on his horse. I was all covered with dirt and blood, for the battle had been fierce and me in the midst of it. But His Excellency seemed not to care about that. Asked me name, he did, and where was I born. 'New Jersey, sir,' I said, 'and of Irish stock, straight from the Emerald Isle.' 'You shall be a soldier, Mistress Hays,' he said, 'and I'll see you never regret your actions here.' Then they notified me I'd had a pension granted—and they took to callin' me Molly Pitcher."

She got up. "I must be off now. I've several miles to go and the night's black. Emmeline, you're a pretty lass. Wouldn't like a job, would you? As pantry-maid? I know where there's such a place."

"In your pantry, Captain Molly?"

"Ah, no, dearie. I've no use for a servant. It's over the river at Robinson's house, where General Arnold is to live with his wife and baby. General Arnold is being made the West Point commander, and Mistress Arnold is a grand lady who must have servants always about her. Major Franks, the General's aide, is at the tavern in Haverstraw, inquirin' for a pantry-maid. I spoke with him there today. If you'd fancy the job, why not try for it? Shall I say a word to the Major, recommending you?"

"Well," Emmeline murmured, and hesitated.

"You can think it over. No hurry. And now I'm leavin'. The tea cheered me, Mistress Drake. May heaven protect and reward you—and don't forget the petticoats . . . Ah, what a queer wall you have here. Muslin, is it?"

"Muslin," Grandmother said. "To cover up the holes."

"And very nice for summer, no doubt. Breezy. But it must be patched before the windy season sets in, eh?"

With a curtsy and a bob of her head, Molly was gone,

and they heard her out in the road again, singing lustily:

> " 'There was Captain Washington
> Upon a slappin' stallion,
> A-givin' orders to his men;
> I guess there was a *million*.' "

The room was silent for a moment after the guest's departure. Then Jed said, "Well, well! So that's Molly Pitcher? She's an odd one."

"She's funny," Kirby said, "and she's mistaken about General Arnold and West Point. Because—"

"Captain Molly is good, *I* think," said Emmeline. "I'm fond of her."

Grandmother folded her sewing and lighted a bedtime candle. "People shouldn't criticize her. She's young; she was married shortly before the war began, and she loved her husband so much that she followed when he went to the army. I suppose she's just waiting now for peace and his returning. I hope he gets back safely and they have many happy years together. Molly is courageous; it's a rare quality in a woman, and I resent the fact that sometimes she's teased and laughed at for occasionally drinking a drop more than she should, or for bragging about her rank and pension."

"But she *is* funny," Kirby insisted.

Grandmother shielded the candle flame. "People think she ought to conduct herself like a lady. That's the funny thing, Kirby. Molly isn't a lady, never was or pretended to be. If she'd been a lady in a frilled cap and a brocade bodice, she'd never have ventured out where the shooting was so thick and fast. Molly's early life didn't make a lady of her— but it made her a strong woman who wouldn't flinch when courage and strength were needed. Fort Clinton couldn't change Molly, or Monmouth, or being hailed as a heroine— and I think that's mostly what people hold against her. But I tell you this, children: Molly Pitcher will be remembered long after the war is over and the victory won, and it won't matter then that these Loyalists in the Hudson Highland have ridiculed her. Molly will be an American legend. I shouldn't wonder if she's written about in history."

"Oh, Granny!" Kirby exclaimed. "In history? Will they have her portrait?"

"Perhaps."

"And *statues?* Will she be wearing her cocked hat and the soldier's jacket?"

Grandmother smiled. "Probably not, Kirby. No, I imagine legend will succeed in making a lady of her. But I'll be proud to stitch Molly's petticoats for her—and maybe if I do them just beautifully, the petticoats will get into the portraits and the statues. Anyway," Grandmother said, "I'd rather sew for Mistress Molly Pitcher Hays than for some others in this neighborhood." She slammed the bureau drawer upon Mr. Joshua Smith's handsome claret silk. "Good night, my dears!"

She kissed them all three, waved her candle emphatically, and went briskly off toward her bedroom.

Kirby was roused by the twitching at his nightgown collar. He knew he had been asleep and that Jed was leaning over him. The window sill beside his cot was ghostly with moonlight.

"Hey! What—"

"Quiet, Kirby. You'll wake Granny. Get up and come outdoors."

"Outdoors? What time is it, for mercy's sake?"

"That's of no consequence. You do as you're told. Emmeline and I have a scheme; we want to talk to you."

"Well, but—hey!"

"You hustle."

"All right," said Kirby, most unwillingly.

4

"I DO SOLEMNLY SWEAR—"

THE MOON WAS HIGH AND RACING WITH A LUMINOUS CLOUD as Kirby crept out of the house. On the bench between the maples Emmeline sat, her blonde hair loose around her neck, a shawl over her nightgown and her feet encased in straw slippers. Jed, still clothed, was sauntering about the yard, as if renewing acquaintance with every tree and shrub it contained.

Kirby slumped down beside Emmeline. "Getting a fellow up in the middle o' the night—"

"Don't grumble." Emmeline threw her arm about his shoulders. "Jed and I have been up for hours."

Jed stopped his aimless prowling and came to squat on his heels beside the bench. "We never went to bed at all, Kirby."

"You said you had a scheme."

"So we have."

"What is your old scheme?" Kirby felt sleepy and abused.

"Granny's birthday," said Jed, "is in October. The third. On that date she'll start for Uncle Tom's."

"She will!" Kirby blinked.

"Yes. She doesn't know it, yet. She'd probably think she couldn't afford the journey—if she thought anything at all about it. But Emmy and I are going to provide the expense money. And you, too, Bud."

"How?" Kirby said. "I don't see—"

"It's like this." Jed plucked a blade of grass which he

thrust between his teeth and chewed pensively. "Each one of us will raise some money—Emmy in her way, you in yours, I in mine. Maybe not so much, but put the three lots together and it's enough. On Granny's birthday, we'll give it all to her; then she can start for Rhode Island and stay there until the war's over."

It sounded simple; but Kirby somehow guessed that it mightn't be. "Would she *go?*"

"We'd have to make her go."

"She wouldn't refuse," Emmeline said, "if she had the money."

"She'd have it," Jed said. "Dumped into her lap. I can understand her love for the cottage. This is our homestead, our land. Our ancestors owned it, the Drakes who emigrated to America more than a century ago. They could have settled anywhere in the new country—"

"But they chose the Hudson," Emmeline said. "They must have liked the bluffs and the glimpses of the river, and the soil and the things they planted in the soil."

"They built the cottage." Jed gestured. "It was home to them. A person's home is—well, it isn't only what he himself puts into it, but what all the family has put into it. Generations of a family, all their dreams and hopes and—and effort. Naturally, Granny wouldn't want to be away forever. None of us would. But I'd never have an easy minute, thinking of her in the cold next winter, with the chimney smoking and the kitchen ready to tumble down!"

"Next winter may not be cold," said Kirby.

"No? A strange winter then, Kirby. You'll have frost by October, at the latest. You yourself told me how bad last winter was."

"It was terrible," said Emmeline.

"And every winter of the war will be a little harder to endure than the one before. I want to think of Granny at

Uncle Tom's farm, snug and comfortable—"

"Where would we get the money?" Kirby was sitting up straight now. "Where in the world?"

"My share," Jed said, "will be my six months' pay that's overdue. Our colonel says we'll have it soon. It's a good deal —or would be if only it was in gold or silver. As things are, we'll be paid in paper. It takes a large amount of paper to make much of a showing. A trunkful of 'continentals' equals a hatful of silver—that's the way to figure it, I suppose. But there are people who buy up the 'continentals,' hoping that they can be redeemed sometime for their true value, or nearly. What I'll do is to trade my paper for silver."

"Can you find somebody to trade with?" Emmeline asked.

"I'll search until I find somebody—and begin searching at once."

"And I'll be a pantry-maid at Robinson's House," said Emmeline. "That was a fine idea of Mistress Molly's. Of course, I've never *been* a pantry-maid, but I'm sure I could be. I think I'll like it and enjoy seeing such a grand, aristocratic lady as Mistress Benedict Arnold. I shall pretend to Grandmother that I'm saving my wages to get warm garments for myself—and, really, I'll be saving them for her . . . Oh, Jed, I do hope General Arnold won't pay his pantry-maid in paper! Is he a rich man?"

"He's not exactly poor. His wife, before her marriage, was Miss Margaret Shippen of Philadelphia. The Shippens are wealthy Loyalists."

"Mistress Arnold's relatives are *Loyalists?*"

"Don't let that disturb you, Emmy. So many Philadelphians are, you know. Why, when Lord Howe occupied the city, the Loyalists held a giant celebration, as if a splendid victory had occurred."

"I suppose they didn't celebrate when the Americans

took back Philadelphia. Well," Emmeline said, "if Mistress Arnold is a Loyalist—"

"But she isn't *now*. She's the wife of a famous American general now, and that makes her an American too." Jed jostled Kirby. "You dozing, Bud? What are you going to do about Granny?"

No, Kirby wasn't dozing. But he didn't know what his part would be in the scheme to send Granny to Uncle Tom's Rhode Island farm. He couldn't be a pantry-maid; no one would give him either a trunkful of "continentals" or a hatful of silver. And there was no work to be had in the neighborhood. At least, not for him. Long ago he had exhausted that possibility. Once he'd said he might enlist in the army as a drummer boy; but Granny wouldn't consent . . . "My gracious!" she had cried. "They've already more drummers than drums to beat!" . . . And he had nothing to sell.

He repeated this now, aloud. "I have nothing to sell—"

"Haven't you?" said Jed.

"Nothing at all."

"Kirby," Emmeline admonished, "think. Think hard."

He thought—and noises issued from the shed behind him: the flapping and fluttering of Emmeline's silly hens, and then a grunting and feeble squeals in a crescendo series.

"No," Kirby said vigorously. *"Nothing."*

"Kirby, dear," Emmeline murmured.

Inside the shed, the gruntings and squeals were varied by sniffs and snorts. Kirby sat even straighter, as if he had a ramrod down his spine.

"I couldn't sell Patience. I love her."

"Maybe not Patience," said Jed. "But all those little porkers."

"I love them too."

"But don't you love Granny more?" coaxed Emmeline. "If you had to decide between a litter of pigs and your own Grandmother—"

"Patience can have a brand-new litter next year," said Jed.

"But these are her first babies," Kirby protested. "She'd be so—so *sad*."

"You mean, you'd be sad. Kirby, you must look at this as a man would—"

"Or a woman," interpolated Emmeline.

"As a grown person," Jed said. "Emmy and I are entering into a solemn, sacred pact to rescue Grandmother—"

"*Rescue* her?"

"That's what it is, really. We know you'll want to join in the partnership. Of course, we may not raise the money, but we'll try to. And if any one of us does succeed, the other two will share the triumph, because it's the trying that counts. And if we all fail—"

"But we won't!" said Emmeline.

"No. We can't . . . Well, Kirby?"

A solemn, secret pact? Kirby mused over that, as the stark white moon shuttled above his head and above the cottage wherein Grandmother was slumbering, all unaware of the conspirators in the yard. He could visualize Granny lying in her bed, her nightcap tied down over her silvery hair and under her chin, her thin hands relaxed on the counterpane. Kirby could not remember his parents, for they had died when he was only a little toddler in pinafores. Since then Granny had been both father and mother to him— and to Emmeline and Jed, too. A very satisfactory Granny. Awfully old, of course (why, she must be sixty-five and maybe more!) but always alert and efficient and capable, always smiling, never whining, scarcely ever scolding—

and then just when scolding was unavoidable. A good, sweet Granny. A *precious* Granny . . .

And all this while Patience was rumbling and loping about in the shed.

"Where can I sell 'em?" Kirby piped at last.

"You dear!" Emmeline kissed him on the tip of his nose.

"Oh, Emmy, *quit!*"

"Brave lad!" said Jed. "Well, you'll have to go to Buttermilk Falls and Haverstraw and Nyack. You may have to cross the river and tramp down as far as North Castle. The taverns, first—"

"Mr. Joshua Smith might like some pigs," said Emmeline, "or General Arnold."

"I'll ask." Kirby nodded. "I'll ask everywhere."

"Before we go in," said Jed, "we must seal this pact with an oath. We'll clasp hands—so! Now say this after me: 'I do hereby solemnly swear to do everything in my power' "—

It was quite a long oath and when Kirby had stumbled through the words, he knew that he was one of an adult partnership with a serious mission. He stood up and told Jed and Emmeline to go on into the house, he would be with them soon.

Alone, he unlocked the door of the shed and stepped inside. A blunt snout brushed against him. He dropped to his knees.

"Here, Patience."

Grandmother had often said that Patience's disposition belied her name; she was a temperamental beast for whom no one but Kirby had ever cherished affection. Now when he stretched out his hand to her, she plunged backward and all the little pigs rushed after her, in fright.

"Patience, I must explain something to you," Kirby whispered

Though she finally sidled up to Kirby, Patience seemed not at all concerned with his explanation, and the little pigs wandered off, too; and at length Kirby got up and let himself out of the shed. At the kitchen door Emmeline was waiting.

"Were you talking to Patience?" she asked.

"I told her about what's going to happen. She didn't act as if she cared."

"She doesn't, and won't. Don't forget, Kirby, that the most attractive animal is never so important as the most unattractive human being."

"What a thing to say! Granny isn't unattractive."

Emmeline laughed. "No, Granny's perfect. And Patience isn't so very attractive, either. Oh, Kirby, I do sympathize with you. Yours will be the biggest sacrifice of all."

"Well, thank you, Emmy."

"Will you do something for me?"

"Something?" He was wary of requests.

"This isn't bad. Will you take me to the village tomorrow—or today, rather, for it's nearly morning now—to see Major Franks at the tavern? Jed would, but he's promised to split kindling for Granny. I'll need you."

"Oh, very well," he said casually. But he was flattered, nonetheless, that Emmy should rely upon him; and he wondered if perhaps this business of selling Patience's offspring might not be quite an adventure, since he would have to jaunt up and down and over the countryside, seeking purchasers.

"Kirby," Emmeline said, "I've just thought: where will *you* be while I'm at Robinson's House and Jed's in the army and Granny is at Uncle Tom's?"

"I'll be here."

"Oh, surely not! By yourself?"

"Someone ought to stay. You know what Jed said, about the Drake homestead."

Emmeline seemed doubtful. "I don't think Jed meant that. And what would you *do,* Kirby?"

"I'd raise pigs. Yes, I shall have this place just full of pigs."

"Mercy! But," Emmeline said, "I suppose that's a bridge we'll cross when we come to it. Good night, Kirby."

"Good night," he said, happily enough.

5

EMMELINE'S VENTURE

THOUGH SHE HAD KEPT SUCH LATE HOURS THE PREVIOUS night, Emmeline wakened with the dawn. She lay and stared up at the ceiling, assembling her thoughts.

What was it she had to do today? Oh, yes! Jumping up, she dressed hurriedly, ran outdoors and was just in time to see the sun bobbing like a huge red melon over the horizon.

There was a moist, cool stillness everywhere, the grass carpeted with glistening dew, the hillsides bathed in coppery green shade, veils of mist swirling in the valleys. The earth gave off damp fragrance, the air was fresh and the sky a vast bowl, gray at first, then lavender which deepened to sheer, clean blue. Emmeline stood a moment in the path, sniffing and tasting the morning. What a wonderful world!

Far off a rooster crowed, and from a greater distance a cannon boomed dully and heavily. Over Emmeline's head a hawk soared and cried raucously. Her enchantment disspelled, Emmeline gathered long skirts about her ankles and ran on to the shed where the hens must be fed and the eggs collected.

When she had finished with these duties, she found that the sun had crept above the tree tops and was painting everything with yellow; cardinals and robins were twittering, and a pair of purple pigeons strutted on the fence and made their little gulping, stuttering announcement that the day was well begun.

Emmeline went into the kitchen. There was a small mirror tacked over the wash bench, and as she washed her hands, she scrutinized her reflection in the wavy surface of the glass. How would she look, to a person wishing to employ a servant? How could she impress an employer with the fact that she was competent and earnest?

"I *think*," she said modestly to herself, "that I'm neat enough, and fairly intelligent looking, too. But do I look *old* enough? My hair is so very light—colorless, like taffy!—and I have no wrinkles, none at all, not even a pucker between my eyebrows. This dimple in my cheek is unfortunate . . . I shall borrow one of Granny's caps. That will make me seem older, and dignified."

She kindled a fire on the hearth, adjusting the short logs so that the smoke would rise properly through the poor, lopsided chimney, and she prepared a cup of tea. She sliced a piece of bread from the loaf, and then carried tea and bread to Grandmother's room, rapping gently on the door.

She had hoped to find Granny not yet out of bed, and she was not disappointed. Granny was wide awake and, seeing Emmeline and the breakfast things, she raised herself on an elbow.

"What's this?" Granny demanded. "You must think I'm sick. I'm not! Breakfast in bed? I never heard of such tomfoolery! It's pure laziness, and it may be sinful! Where did you get such a notion?"

Emmeline was somewhat taken aback. "I read it in a book. A queen, or maybe she was only a countess—at any rate, she had her tea brought to the bedside. I thought you might like it, just once. I suppose Mistress Arnold always has her breakfast so."

"Mistress Arnold? I daresay she does."

Emmeline set the cup and plate on the little table. "I'm—I'm rather clumsy."

"No, not at all." As Emmeline blushed, Granny said: "Well, it's very nice. Yes, indeed. A queen in a book, eh? You'll spoil me with this luxury—which would be a pity, at my age. Sit down here, my dear." Her eyes were twinkling. "So you've been thinking of what Captain Molly told you?"

Emmeline sat on the edge of the bed. "Yes, I have."

"You want to be a maid at Robinson's House?"

"If—if you have no objections, Granny?"

"The truth is, I've been thinking of that very thing."

"Oh!"

"Yes," Granny said. "I'll miss having you at home; but this may be an opportunity to earn money with which to clothe yourself, and perhaps even a bit to put aside for the rainy days that come to all of us."

Emmeline nodded, and felt guilty as Granny spoke of what might be done with her earnings. But her feeling of relief was even stronger, for she had feared that Granny might oppose the plan.

"I wouldn't let you go as a domestic servant in ordinary times; you wouldn't have to," Granny was saying. "But these are war times and therefore not ordinary. Somehow, war makes everything topsy-turvy, doesn't it? No order anywhere, no system. War affects not only the lives of soldiers, but of every person in the country. It's like an octopus, reaching out, gripping, smothering all the good—destroying. Dear, dear!" Granny wagged her head. "Maybe if historians would write less about the glory and the conquering, and more about the suffering, we'd have fewer wars."

Emmeline smiled and seemed to listen, but she was really thinking of what she would wear to the village. Her brown frock? It was the newest one, a gift from Uncle Tom and the Rhode Island cousins last Christmas. But the sprigged muslin, with a white fichu and fluting at the neck, was prettier.

"And Granny's cap, the round one, with the embroidery ruffle. And I'll wear my mitts, too, and carry a linen handkerchief." . . .

Emmeline walked sedately through the summer afternoon. Behind her Kirby scuffed and darted, like an inquisitive puppy, swerving off now and again to chase a squirrel or chipmunk. They skirted the lane which led to the ferry and the fortress where, more than a year ago, on July 15, 1779, General Anthony Wayne had won his smashing victory.

The story of that battle was one of which Kirby never tired.

"Let me tell it to you, Emmeline—"

"But I've heard it. Often."

"Well, anyway," Kirby said, and without more preface he told it.

General Wayne, Kirby said, had vowed to storm Stony Point and to wrest it from English possession—no matter what the costs or hazards. To that end he had drilled his regiment of Massachusetts light infantry, and marched them by companies through narrow defiles, across lowlands, massing them in rendezvous a mile and a half below the fortress.

Situated on the rocky bluff, and bordered by the marsh and barricades of piled-up timber, it seemed too much a stronghold ever to be taken. But with nightfall, Wayne had moved forward, guided by Pompey, a Negro slave from the neighborhood. Wayne put all his trust in Pompey—for the old black bondman knew a way to get into the fortress!

Pompey also knew the enemy's countersign. All summer he had gone in and out of the British lines, peddling cherries and berries to the garrison. The Britishers thought Pompey stupid, just a pedlar; they teased and patronized him; and they were such eager customers that they gave him the countersign, so that he could pass the pickets at any hour, day or night.

And on the night of July 15—

"It was eleven-thirty, Emmy," Kirby said. "Very hot, pitch-dark—and *still*. All the dogs around here had been killed by our fellows the day before. All of them. That was bad, wasn't it? I should hate to kill a dog. Dogs are such nice creatures. But, of course, they might have barked, and General Wayne couldn't have risked the alarm. Well, Pompey went ahead, and with him were two soldiers disguised as farmers, in jeans and farm hats, you know. When the first sentinel challenged, Pompey said. 'It's only me. Pompey.' And he repeated the countersign, 'The fort's our own.' The sentinel stood aside, and then the two 'farmers' leaped on him and gagged and bound him. So much for that sentinel. Pompey went to the next one. They gagged and bound him, too."

"Meanwhile," said Emmeline, "the tide had ebbed, and Wayne was treading over the quaking marsh—"

"No! Let *me* tell it! . . . Wayne and his forces weren't seen, not even *seen*, Emmy, until they were within pistol range. Then somebody did see them, somebody yelled, 'To arms, to arms!' And the fife was blown and the drums rolled. But the Americans were too close by that time, and too many. Each of our men had a strip of white paper in his hat, you know, so they wouldn't accidentally shoot their comrades. They struck down the British standard and they raised our flag. They rushed about, shouting, '*The fort's our own!*' And it was! Before daybreak Stony Point surrendered, the King's troops were prisoners, and General Wayne was dispatching his message to George Washington."

"I can quote you the message," Emmeline said. "'The fort and garrison are ours . . . Our officers and men behaved like men who are determined to be free.' That's what Wayne wrote to Washington."

"And now he's called Mad Anthony! Mad Anthony Wayne!"

"You're capering as though you were mad yourself, Kirby."

"It's thinking of Stony Point!" Kirby turned an agile handspring.

"But you must calm down, for there's the tavern. Oh, I do hope I'll not forget my manners! Do I look all right, Kirby? Am I all dusty?"

"You look good enough. Don't be such a scared-cat." Then Kirby was suddenly protective. "I'll sit out on the hitch-rail and if anyone's rude to you, just you call me, Emmy."

The proprietor said that General Arnold wasn't in the tavern; he had ridden off during the forenoon and hadn't yet returned. But Major Franks was in the small chamber adjoining the taproom. Emmeline rapped timidly on the taproom door, which was opened by a young man of medium height and military bearing.

"Major Franks?"

"Yes." He had a pleasant, tanned face and a saber scar on his jaw. "What can I do for you?"

With some embarrassment, Emmeline told who she was and what was her errand.

"This is a matter I know little about," Major Franks said. "You'll have to consult Mistress Catherine Martin, the Arnolds' housekeeper. Mistress Martin is here in the tavern. Pray be seated while I summon her." Bowing slightly, the Major went out and his bootheels clicked in the corridor.

After a moment a woman entered the room. She was short and plump, her stout waist girdled by an apron so starchy that it crackled as she walked. On her brown hair she wore a butterfly cap, with streamers; a scarf of snowy lawn was knotted at her throat. Everything about her was as spotless as soap and water could have made it, and the hand she extended to Emmeline looked red and rough, as if it had just been scoured.

"I'm Catherine Martin. You wished to speak with me?"

"Well," Emmeline said, "I suppose it's useless—now. If Major Franks has hired you, he will have hired any other servants General Arnold needs. I had thought I might be the pantry-maid—"

"And what's to hinder you?" queried Mistress Martin crisply. "I haven't just been hired. Not at all. I've kept General Arnold's house ever since he married Miss Shippen. I daresay the Arnolds couldn't get along without me"

"Oh! And *are* you wanting a pantry-maid?"

"I certainly am. Badly wanting. Robinson's House is big. I couldn't do everything myself. Mistress Arnold takes a deal of waiting on; and there's the baby, too. We'll have soldiers for the chores in the garden and stables; but I'm to look for a kitchen-helper. The only thing General Arnold asks of me is that it all runs smooth as glass and Mistress Arnold is spared the worrying. And what training have you had in service?"

"None, Mistress Martin."

"Oh, address me as Catherine. Why, I'm but twenty-five, not so much older than you, for all I'm so fat! You've never worked before?"

"Just at home. Never for anyone else."

"But are you industrious?"

"I—I think I am."

"Would you be conscientious?"

"Yes," Emmeline said. "I would."

"Wages? Will you accept what's usual?"

Emmeline smiled. "I don't know what is usual. Anything you think right will suit me."

"That's good. No haggling. I never like it." Catherine Martin regarded Emmeline appraisingly. "You're very comely, with your blonde braids and blue eyes. I hope you're not one to have your head turned by the silly flattery of any boys who might be hanging around."

Emmeline's smile faded; crimson dyed her cheeks. "No boys are hanging around. Not ever! My grandmother wouldn't allow it."

"So you've been strictly reared?"

"Yes, I have."

"Well, I think you'll do, Emmeline, and that you and I will hit it off nicely. I'll tell you something about your tasks."

As Emmeline listened attentively, Catherine Martin instructed her in the routine expected of a pantry-maid—"though," Catherine said, "you can't know much about it until we're there, at the house." She told something about herself, also. She was the wife of a soldier, a sergeant major in a Pennsylvania regiment; she had been married for several years and was devoted to her husband; when the war separated them she welcomed the chance to go into service for such distinguished personages as the Arnolds. She had known Major Franks a long time, too, and respected him.

She did not anticipate with much pleasure this removal to the Hudson Highlands.

"A wild country. I declare, I don't see how my delicate, fastidious lady will ever stand it! The house may be a mansion, but it's quite off, in the forest, Major Franks says, with no other residences for miles around and none of the parties and balls and society excitement that Mistress Arnold craves, none of the conveniences she's used to. Well, we'll just have to make her as happy as we can. And now, Emmeline, you go home and pack your things."

"I haven't many things to pack."

Catherine said: "All the better, since you must be rowed over that river! I'll look for you then on the fourth of the month. In the afternoon?"

"In the afternoon." To herself, Emmeline was saying jubilantly: "I have a job! I really have! I'm doing my share in the solemn pact!"

The thought was still uppermost in her mind when she went out of the tavern. She passed Major Franks at the tap-room door. Kirby was sitting on the hitch-rail and down the road, a horseman galloped, puffs of dust whirling from the pounding hoofs.

The horseman pulled up before the tavern and vaulted from the saddle. Major Franks ran forward, stopped and brought his spurs together, saluting.

" 'Evening, Franks."

"Good evening, General."

"I've done it!" The General was smiling, yanking off his gloves. "We have the post at West Point."

"That is scarcely news, sir."

"The devil it isn't! When I reached Tappan, there it was in the bulletin for the day. I'd been assigned to the field, the left wing, active duty. But I argued—and now we go to Robinson's House. You must send to Philadelphia for bedding, china, silver, all the things which Mistress Arnold will like in that gloomy palace yonder."

Major Franks' tanned countenance had assumed a puzzled look. "I've done that, sir. Catherine Martin and I proceeded on your directions given weeks ago, while we were yet in Pennsylvania. You said then that you would command West Point."

"Yes, I did. And I will."

"I hadn't thought there was any question about it."

"Nor is there. I shall command West Point. 'Egad! I trust no rumor of this has got to Mistress Arnold, or she'll be distressed. You think, Franks, some idiot may say to her that I'm *not* to have West Point?"

"I don't know, sir." Major Franks seemed constantly more baffled. "As for myself, I believed what you told me."

"A commendable trait, Major Franks! Well, then, we go to Robinson's House!"

There was a rustling which was Kirby getting down from the hitch-rail. "General Arnold?" said Kirby.

"Yes? What is it?"

"Would you like to buy five little pigs, sir?"

"Pigs?" The General's flashing black eyes surveyed the boy. "No, I would not."

"Would you like to buy one little pig, sir?"

"No, I would not."

"They'd be nice pets, sir, or—" Kirby gulped—"you *could* eat them."

"Don't bother me with your talk of pigs." General Arnold's arm went up. "Begone, urchin!" His arm descended, and the gloves which he held in his hand swiped a mark of startling paleness across Kirby's forehead. And Kirby sprang back, his fist clenched angrily.

"Kirby!" Emmeline cried.

He turned and saw her; and in that brief instant General Arnold walked away into the tavern. Behind him was Major Franks; and Emmeline thought that she saw in the Major's eyes the shadow of regret at his superior officer's show of temper.

"It was unintentional, Kirby," Emmeline said, as they

went homeward. "A miscalculation; he wouldn't have hit you. General Arnold's a great man, a famous man. Probably if you got to know him, you'd admire him."

"I don't believe I *want* to know him, Emmy."

"You don't have to."

But Emmeline reflected that *she* would know General Arnold, for in three more days, she would begin service in his household.

6

JOURNEY AND ARRIVAL

"I THINK WE'VE REMEMBERED EVERYTHING," GRANDMOTHER said, as she handed Emmeline a steaming porringer. "Your bundle of clothing is all tied up, and the lunch wrapped in a napkin. Now, my dear, you sit down and eat a bite. Jed will be around presently with the wagon."

Emmeline looked at the bundle and tried to smile, but her mouth twisted and her chin quivered. She felt chilled through, her fingers like icicles, her knees unsteady. This was another morning—and she was leaving all the dear, familiar things of home.

Granny seemed not to notice Emmeline's evidences of nervousness, but was even more brisk than usual, tripping about from hearth to table and keeping up a flow of conversation.

"It was an inspiration of Jed's, to borrow Mr. Brinsley's horse for the day. The journey's such a long one, you'd have been exhausted before you got to the landing stage. This way, you can go in style. I declare, I almost envy you. It'll be like having a picnic, with your noon meal under the trees."

"I wish you and Kirby were going, Granny."

"Yes, and we might, except that I'm so busy. Mr. Joshua Smith is wanting his silk coat. I've skimped my work since Jed's been here. I'm glad he's to go with you; it's only right he should. The country is rugged, and you never know when those cowboys will come roistering down the road, waylaying cattle and supplies intended for our army and making mischief for travelers. Cowboys, indeed! They're nothing but Loyalist ruffians and rowdies!"

"Aren't the skinners ruffians too, Granny?"

"Yes, they are, though they claim to be patriots, young men and boys from families that believe in the rebellion and support the Continental Congress. The skinners say that the Loyalist cowboys started all this thieving and petty bandit warfare on the roads and at bridges and culverts, and that the skinners had to band together to protect the patriot farmers. But the skinners are often mischievous, too. I've little use for either the cowboys *or* the skinners."

Emmeline sat, listlessly eating her gruel, looking about, realizing how much she loved the cottage, how dear it was to her.

"Where's Kirby, Granny?"

"He's out feeding Patience and her children. Kirby thinks you'll want to bid Patience a formal farewell."

Now Emmeline did smile. "I don't exactly want to. But I will, if Kirby would like it."

She got up and went into the yard where Kirby had herded the six pigs. While he watched and Grandmother stood by, Emmeline curtsied elaborately to Patience and her brood. Then the borrowed wagon clattered into sight, with Jed at the reins.

Emmeline's eyes met Grandmother's.

"I'll not tell you goodbye," she said huskily. "If you don't mind, I'll just pretend I'm going for a few hours."

"That's best," agreed Grandmother.

Grasping Jed's hand, Emmeline hoisted herself over the wheel, deposited her bundle in the wagon-bed and sat down beside her brother.

"Gee," said Jed to the horses. "Hie on with you."

Not until they were at the bend in the road, did Emmeline glance back. Then, as she saw Granny and Kirby through a gap in the hedge, she brushed a tear from her cheek. But she saw also the east wall of the cottage, the defective chimney; and she thought of how the wind would howl through the valley in December, the relentless winter wind which Granny must escape. And the sadness of this morning was simply a part of the escape, a sadness which would at last be remedied, when Emmeline came home again.

The road wound around the base of Donderberg Mountain and Bear Hill and then followed the Hudson's shore. At first Jed and Emmeline were quiet, but as Fort Clinton and Fort Montgomery came in view, Jed began to speak about the war.

It had always been the desire of the British, he said, to seize the territory which flanked the river and thus split in two the resistance of the defiant colonies. Burgoyne had tried that, and had been sternly rebuffed at Saratoga. But in the autumn of 1777, ten days before the battle of Saratoga, the British had successfully attacked Fort Clinton and Fort Montgomery.

"Right here," Jed said, gesturing, "we had some ships, two frigates, two galleys and an armed sloop. When the forts were taken, the crews of the vessels spread sails, slipped cables and would have made a dash for it, upstream. But the wind was against them, so they set the ships afire to prevent their falling into the hands of the enemy. What a spectacle that must have been, Emmy!"

"Yes!" In imagination Emmeline witnessed it—the flames spurting forth, growing, flaring up and up, until all this area between the bluffs was filled with red light and the water reflected the weird, unnatural glow. The loaded cannon on the ships' decks had exploded with a noise mightier than thunder, and with that detonation the craft had sunk beneath the water, the scarlet fury had faded from sky and bluffs, and the night was abruptly black and soundless.

"The enemy," Jed said, "had the forts, but after Burgoyne's surrender they weren't of much benefit and were soon abandoned. The British will never give up the ambition to get control of the Hudson, though, and make a clear passage southward for their reinforcements in Canada. Now that they're occupying New York City, they probably think of coming up the river again. That's why West Point is so important. While we have it, we can block that passage. A lot depends on our holding West Point. If it were lost, the whole war might be lost."

"Oh, Jed! We won't lose the war. We'll win!"

"Yes, because we simply have to."

"Granny says because God is with us."

"I think that." He nodded somberly. "Every patriot thinks that. This year has been discouraging, we've had reverses; there's grumbling among people both in and out of the army."

"But the French are our allies now."

"And we have General Washington. Yes, it may take a long time, but we'll win—finally."

"Jed," Emmeline said, after a pause, "what's your opinion of General Arnold?"

"*My* opinion? As if it mattered!"

"No, tell me."

"I don't know much about him. In battle, they say, he's a lion, reckless and daring. Everybody praises him for it."

"Is he popular with his men?"

"Oh, so-so. Not popular as some of the other officers are—Washington and Mad Anthony Wayne and Lafayette. Arnold has a temper, he can be arrogant and overbearing to his inferiors in rank. And there was the court-martial at Philadelphia—"

"I heard Kirby asking Grandmother about that."

"Kirby?"

"He'd got hold of the tale somewhere. But Granny wouldn't say much, except that scandal should be allowed to die—and that little pitchers have wide ears."

"Sounds like Granny." Jed grinned. "Well, the court-martial was a pretty serious affair. After the British evacuated the city, Washington put Arnold in command there, to preserve order and protect the civilians and their property. The civilians had been badly used by the British, you know. Arnold moved in and set up headquarters. Not long afterward, he married Miss Shippen. She's his second wife; his first wife had been dead for several years. People soon became suspicious of General Arnold—"

"Why? Because Miss Shippen was a Loyalist?"

"I suppose they did whisper about that. Mostly, though, it was his extravagance. He lived like a lord!—and when everybody else was poor as poverty. After a while, the Pennsylvania Council was accusing him of selling the goods and food of private citizens and pocketing the profits."

"Oh, Jed! No one would do *that*."

"You wouldn't think so, would you? They said he was overfriendly with Philadelphians who were known to be Tories and granted them favors, and that he used public conveyances for his own conveniences. He had displeased the council in so many ways that they had him tried by court-martial. Some of the charges were dropped, I believe; but on two counts the court found him guilty. Arnold was bitter about it—"

"I can imagine!" Emmeline said softly.

"What?"

"Oh, nothing. Go on, Jed."

"Well, he left Philadelphia and the army, and stayed at his estate in Mount Pleasant, with his sister and his three sons by his first marriage. He's been there all the time—until General Washington assigned him to West Point."

As they jogged on, Emmeline thought of telling Jed of her single glimpse of Benedict Arnold, but she decided against it. She hadn't spoken of it to Grandmother, and Kirby had said nothing. Jed would only be worried. And perhaps a man so vexed and burdened as General Arnold should be pardoned for outbursts of impatience.

"I mustn't be prejudiced," Emmeline again said to herself. "I'll not judge him hastily. He may really be very kind. And probably Kirby *was* a bother—though he never seems so to me . . . Dear Kirby!"

Jed had caught the sound of a little sigh; he looked curiously down at her. "Penny for your thoughts. You're not homesick? Not so soon?"

"If I am homesick, it's just a bit." She squeezed his arm. "And you haven't a penny."

At noon, driving into the tiny village of Buttermilk Falls, they saw Mistress Molly Pitcher sauntering at the roadside. She was attired in her military costume, a sergeant's stripe on her sleeve and the peaked hat at a jaunty angle. Delighted, Jed and Emmeline stopped.

"Mistress Molly," Emmeline announced, "I'm going to Robinson's House."

"Are you now! You got the place?"

"Yes, thanks to you."

Molly leaned against the wagon. "Ah, it was nothing. I wish I were goin' with you. I don't like it here. Not at all. I've the notion to shake the dust of Buttermilk Falls from me feet. These folks—they haven't the proper regard for me. Treat me like dirt, they do. But I'll show 'em!" She flounced her skirts and tossed her auburn head. "Some day I'll walk off—an' where'll they be then, eh? No Captain Molly! No Mistress Hays, with a pension an' medals from

General Washington, himself! I'll walk off—an' the back o' me hand to 'em all!"

"Why don't you walk down to Grandmother's?" Emmeline said.

"Maybe I will. I could do worse. Well, rare luck to you, dearie, over the river. An' have a care not to get a leaky skiff an' wet that neat little cape you have around you!"

As Molly strolled on, Jed maneuvered the creaking wagon down the slope to the landing stage. Grandmother had said they must tether Mr. Brinsley's horse, rent a rowboat and so cross the river. Disembarking on the east bank, they could eat their lunch at Beverley Dock and then go on foot the three-quarters of a mile to Robinson's House.

When the boat was procured, Emmeline climbed in; Jed pushed off and grasped the oars. The current was swift; for a moment he tussled with it, but soon he was sending the unwieldy skiff over the water with long, strong strokes.

The noon sun was hot as they beached; a breeze rippled the rusty foliage of the trees under which they sat, to investigate the contents of the lunch packet. Jed ate with normal appetite, but Emmeline only sampled the food. She had a hollow sensation in the pit of her stomach, and as her eyes rested on Jed's bare brown head and bronzed face, she dreaded to part from him.

"You must not be hungry," he said.

"No, I'm not—somehow."

"Excitement, I guess. Well, Emmy, come on, old girl."

Reluctantly she got up and accompanied him along the willow-shaded lane.

Robinson's House was known to all inhabitants of the Hudson Highlands, for its owner, Colonel Beverley Robinson, was a man of prominence. Before the outbreak of war, Robinson had been a friend of George Washington's—though he objected to the colonists' policies, at first mildly and then more strenuously. He said there was no reason for the war, and after war became a fact and arguing against it was of no more avail, and after he had quarreled with Washington and other patriots, Robinson retired to his country estate, thinking it would be quite possible for him to live in seclusion, ignoring the war and never being asked embarrassing questions by his neighbors.

But he had reckoned without the oath of allegiance to the state which he was asked to take. Beverley Robinson balked at that. No, he would not swear a loyalty which he did not feel. He was a Loyalist of another type. Thereafter, his existence was made increasingly difficult and his neighbors referred to him as a traitor.

As a result of the local unpleasantness, Robinson left the Highlands and sought refuge in New York City, where now he was an officer in a regiment of the King's troops. Probably this decision was a happy one for all concerned; Robinson himself had not regretted it, and his home had been converted by the Americans into a headquarters for the West Point commandant.

The house was just at the foot of Sugar Loaf Mountain. The big rambling structure was painted white, with a steep roof and tall, slender pillars on the veranda. There was a spacious lawn where trees were planted in rows and garden flowers had been arranged in geometrical beds—and then neglected. On two sides of the lawn were forests and behind the house the mountains were dark and frowning.

As Jed and Emmeline neared, Catherine Martin came out onto the veranda. She was apron-clad and vigorously shaking a dust-rag. The windows had been raised, with rugs hung to air over the sills. A broom, a mop and a bucket of soapy water were on the front steps and from the chimneys smoke curled in purple spirals.

Behind the house the mountains were dark and frowning

"Hello, hello!" Catherine said. "So here you are. And this is your brother?"

Jed bowed to her. "You must have arrived early, ma'am."

"Yes, and I've been busy as a beaver. Yet I've scarce made a dent in the dust and dirt. Such an accumulation! And the mice have taken over, as if it were their own homestead! I'm relieved to see you, Emmeline, for I'd have been loath to spend the night alone. A desolate place this is, and the last *I'd* ever pick to build a mansion in!"

"It's been the scene of many a gay entertainment," Emmeline said. "Colonel Robinson was a great host."

Catherine looked skeptical. "Those rocks, that old Sugar Loaf—and the *thunder!*"

"Oh, that's nothing."

"Maybe not. But it fair gives me the shivers. What my lady will do here, I really can't picture. Have a fit of hysterics, likely—as she often does."

"Hysterics? What's that?"

"Have you never seen a person in hysterics, Emmeline? Weeping and moaning and laughing? Perhaps you'll have the chance. I sometimes think Mistress Arnold is just playacting and the seizures are her way of getting everyone to pity her and toe the mark. And everyone does . . . But there! I may be wrong. Mistress Arnold's been brought up like a little princess; it's probably not her fault if she flies off the handle when things don't just suit her. *I* wouldn't, and you wouldn't, either, for we're taught to be mannerly. If ever *I* had hysterics, a pail of cold water would be doused in my face, and that would be the end of that! But rich folks—well, you know how they are."

Emmeline did not know. Her experience with the rich was limited, and she would have enjoyed prolonging the conversation.

But Catherine was brandishing her dust-rag and bustling

back into the house, saying as she went that **Mistress Arnold** had expressly wanted to live here, that she and the General had talked only of West Point and its many opportunities.

"Opportunities for *what,* I'd like to know!" said Catherine. "To go raving crazy, perhaps!"

Jed, after greeting Mistress Martin, had strolled about the premises; now he came to the veranda and said he must be off. This was his last day of furlough and he had promised to spend the evening with Grandmother.

"I don't think Catherine is pleased, Jed," observed Emmeline.

"Are you?" he asked.

"The house does give me the shivers, too—a little."

"You needn't stay, Emmy."

"But our partnership, our oath, and getting Granny to Rhode Island?"

"Kirby and I might arrange that."

"No, I want to be in it! I'll stay."

"You'll be among interesting people, Emmy. That will console you. It's what I tell myself when I feel homesick at my soldiering. 'Jed Drake,' I say, 'history is in the making and you've a part in it!' The same is true of life at Robinson's House. You keep your eyes and ears open, Emmy; and you may be astonished at how much you learn here."

"Thank you, Jed," said Emmeline, and kissed him.

But she did not dream, as she saw him stride away, how completely his prophecy would be fulfilled.

7

JED MAKES A TOUR

JED DID NOT GO DIRECTLY HOME, AFTER ALL.

At the dock he met Rawlins, a fisherman from Buttermilk Falls, whose dinghy had run aground on a hidden shoal and been so disabled that its owner could not revisit the nets he had spread that morning at Martalaer's Rock and at West Point. If Jed would row him to these nets, the fisherman would divide the evening's catch with him.

"A fine mess of perch for your supper, eh?" said Rawlins temptingly.

"Done!" Jed exclaimed, envisaging the delight of Grandmother and Kirby when he should bring them such a prize.

The skiff was swung into the shallows and then headed upstream. Rawlins, a cordial fellow, was not averse to taking a turn at the oars; and so, within a half-hour, they had pulled up to Martalaer's Rock. While the nets were being drawn and emptied, Jed glanced about him.

It was upon this protruding finger of granite-ribbed land that the first fortifications of the Hudson had been erected, for here the river was at its narrowest and running at an abrupt east-west course, with the opposite shore quite close. In the autumn of 1775, at Washington's insistence, the fort at Martalaer's Rock had been begun; but so quickly was the construction carried on and so perishable were the materials used that the barricades and batteries were never practical; and when Forts Clinton and Montgomery fell, the efforts at Martalaer's were given up as a bad job and relinquished. Now, after five years of wind and weather, there remained on the peninsula only the skeletons of crumbling walls and heaps of stone and rubble.

But Martalaer's Rock still had a purpose. In a sheltered redoubt on the shore was fastened one end of the great chain which had been stretched from the newer fortifications at West Point across the river as an obstruction to any British ships which might attempt to go up the Hudson toward Canada.

That chain was a source of wonder to all New Yorkers.

"Haven't you seen it before?" Rawlins asked, as Jed looked at the great spool upon which the chain could be wound.

"Oh, yes. But I'd like to see it again. Big, isn't it?"

"Big? That's not the word. Why, that chain weighs one hundred and eighty tons! The links were forged at a foundry twenty-five miles from West Point—best foundry in America!—and hauled by teamsters over there on the west bank."

"Was it put together on the West Point side?"

"Yes. And a labor it was, too! Then they strung it across the Hudson, just under the surface of the water. But that's not all of it. Underneath there's a second chain—of logs, linked and hooked together; the boom, it's called. You can't see the boom, but if you were steering a vessel through here—well, you'd feel it! The boom and chain would stop you mighty quick, and there you'd be, your hull pricked like a sieve. And pretty soon you'd be right at the bottom of the river."

"Our leaders seem to think the boom and chain will keep the British from navigating the Hudson."

"It ought to keep them from *trying*." Rawlins grinned. "Though they say Sir Henry Clinton, the British commander at New York, would give his eyes to take West

Point—and he might be fool enough to chance it! He has that sloop, the *Vulture,* down at Kingsbridge, and every now and then there's a little flurry, with the *Vulture* coming up a few miles—and dropping back again. Well, shall we go over and see the other end of the boom and chain contraption?"

They rowed to West Point, to the redoubt which was the twin of the one on Martalaer's Rock. Above it were barracks and huts, embankments of logs and earth, all fortifications which had been begun by General Kosciuzko, the gallant Polish officer, who was the first to command here.

Jed thought that West Point, with its enormous quantities of powder, munitions and military supplies, must surely be impregnable. Except from the dock, the post could not be approached; behind it, in the hills, were Forts Putnam, Webb, and Wyllys and numerous smaller ambuscades; and, as if to aid in the reinforcements, nature had gashed the hills with gulleys and thrown up clusters of stone which ridged the dense forests and the thorn-barbed undergrowth.

"I've heard," remarked Rawlins, "there are near three thousand troops in this garrison."

"And everyone needed, I suppose."

"Yes. West Point was undermanned a while ago, until General Benedict Arnold inspected it, in June. The soldiers then didn't have enough guns or provisions; they had no flour or sugar or meat. But things are better now."

"Was that General Arnold's doing, getting the extra men and the guns and food?"

"Well, it may have been, and may not. Anyway, I think as most people do, that General Arnold's going to be a good commandant. West Point is safe with such an officer in charge, and so long as the post's safe, the country hereabout is, too."

This was almost precisely what Jed himself had said to Emmeline, and he nodded. "The post could be taken by just one means. If a link in the chain were broken—"

"Ah, but that could never happen!" Rawlins laughed. "Why, it's kept in condition, examined—often! No, no, my lad." He paused. "Now you say West Point could be taken by just one means, and I'll not deny that. But it would have to be by treachery. Suppose the post should be sold out to Sir Henry Clinton, delivered to him, lock, stock and barrel? Have you ever thought of that?"

"No, I haven't. And it's an absurd thing to think about. Sold out? By whom?" Jed was indignant. "Where's the traitor so black as to do that?"

"Oh, I'm not saying it will happen—for I know it won't. But I'm saying it *could* happen. I'm no Loyalist, and you needn't be glaring at me so. But I've lived in these parts all my life and during the war years I've seen many a strange and stealthy action and many a man who talked like a patriot and behaved like a Tory snake-in-the-grass. The British have money; don't forget that; and there are some people who will do anything for money. The root of all evil! Sir Henry Clinton may put it out as bait here and there—as I cast out worms and crawdads for my fish— hoping for a nibble."

"He'll not get a nibble!"

"I'm not saying he will."

"He won't!"

"Well, you and I mustn't fuss about it, eh?"

Jed was abashed. "No, we'll not fuss. Only, God forbid that there ever should be such a nibble!"

"Amen," breathed Rawlins piously.

Sped by the current, they went toward Buttermilk Falls; and before sunset Jed was climbing into Mr. Brinsley's wagon and waving his hand to Rawlins who folded his nets on the landing stage.

"Gee!" said Jed, to the horse. "Giddap!"

Across the water he could glimpse the outline of Beverley Dock, with its leaning willows. He thought of Emmeline and sent her his silent good wishes. What a splendid girl she was, a sister to be proud of. He hoped that she would be content at Robinson's House—and he knew that the family there would like her! Everyone liked Emmy; she was gentle, clever and sweet.

Jed's furlough would be over in a few hours now. Tomorrow he would resume the grim business of soldiering again. He would put on the uniform which Granny had been darning and mending, and the cumbersome boots. Over his shoulder he'd sling the knapsack, the blanket, the haversack of rations; and to his belt he'd clip his canteen, the hatchet, his sidearms and bullet pouch. He would take up his musket. And thus loaded with sixty pounds of equipment, he would march and march.

With luck, there might perhaps be days or weeks when he would have a mount and be detailed as a courier, carrying messages to other camps; or he might be patrolling, or dispatched into the forest with a squad of engineers to clear a road or bridge a creek. In war you never know what the next day will hold, because you must yield to someone else's will.

Jed detested war. And yet there was a kind of satisfaction about being a soldier, a feeling he couldn't have defined. Every man, every boy, in the army knew that he was doing his share to win the blessings of peace. War was, perhaps, like the phoenix in the story which Grandmother once had told him, a burning, a destruction, a waste, with something shining and beautiful rising from the ashes.

Now the sun was down. Jed glanced back into the wagon-bed where seven fish were covered with green leaves. Granny would broil those perch and they would be very tasty.

"Two for Granny, two for me—and three for Kirby, the greedy rascal! Hie on, my bonny," said Jed to Mr. Brinsley's old gray mare.

8

VISITOR TO ROBINSON'S HOUSE

WHEN EMMELINE HAD BEEN A FULL WEEK AT ROBINSON'S House, Catherine Martin handed her a silver half-crown.

"Your wages," Catherine said, "for the fortnight. Of course, I needn't have paid you in advance, but I notice you haven't so much as a penny; and since Major Franks has given me the money for household expenditures, I can let you have this now. I wouldn't do so if I didn't know that you'll make a very good pantry-maid and I'll have no cause to complain of you."

Emmeline stared at the silver coin, turning it over in her palm. A half-crown each fortnight, a whole crown each month—that seemed quite a lot!

"You must not squander it, Emmeline."

"Oh, no! I shall save it. I've a special reason. May I run upstairs and put it away?" As Catherine nodded, Emmeline started for the door, and paused. "Thank you for saying that I've pleased you."

"Well, you have." Catherine was matter-of-fact. "You may be sure I'd not say so unless I meant it."

Emmeline went up to her small chamber which was on the second floor, under the eaves. She slipped the coin into the pocket of her sprigged muslin frock and then thrust the frock back into a corner of the high walnut wardrobe. She locked the wardrobe and placed the key under the strip of rug beside her cot. Then she lay down on the cot, propped herself on an elbow, and gazed out the single window toward Sugar Loaf Mountain, hazy and blue-green in the distance.

It was afternoon, an hour when a lull occurred in the routine of chores—and one of the infrequent hours of leisure granted her since her coming to Robinson's House. As she thought of the seven days just elapsed, she knew that they hadn't been easy ones; they had been difficult, with everything so strange and so much to learn and remember.

She was gratified that Catherine Martin should praise her, even a mite, for by this time she knew Catherine to be a person who would not indulge in idle words. She felt that she had made a friend of Catherine—and Emmeline thought such a friend worth having! Robinson's House was still rather oppressive, with a queer air of loneliness about it, as if it waited for dramatic and perhaps sinister happenings.

If Catherine had one dominant characteristic, it was (so Emmeline thought) thoroughness. Whatever Catherine did, she did as perfectly as was possible, throwing herself heart and soul into the work and never stopping until she had achieved results. When Catherine scrubbed a floor, the wooden boards emerged from her scrub-brush so immaculate that you could have eaten your supper off them; when she washed a window, each pane sparkled; in the surface of the tables she polished, you could see the unblemished reflection of your face.

It was in this thorough fashion that she had cleaned Robinson's House, overhauling each room, going from ceiling to wainscot. Her supply of energy seemed as endless as her supply of soap; and all the while that she herself was so industrious, she kept a critical eye on her assistant. At home, Emmeline had been wont to glide through the cleaning process; to sit down when she became tired, to quit entirely if the impulse struck her, to drift out to the cupboard for an apple, a seed-cake, or any snack of food, or for a cool drink from the bucket. But with Catherine supervising, there was none of this frivolity. No, indeed! Catherine did not scold; she was not irritable. She merely looked candidly at you—and so, from sunup to sundown, you worked!

Emmeline had formed some conclusions during these seven days. She believed that to occupy such an establishment as this would be more of a burden than a joy. She couldn't imagine why anyone would wish to be laden with as many possessions as, apparently, the Arnolds had, or how they could endure so complicated an existence. Once she had thought it would be lovely to be rich; now she was positive that a simple life, like the one she had known always in the Drakes' cottage, was better. When she should marry and have a home of her own (as she hoped some day to do) she would want that home to be just like the cottage!

"And no servants," said Emmeline. "Not any. Indeed, after this training with Catherine Martin, there'll not be anything I can't do for myself."

The afternoon was sultry with August heat, but Emmeline felt quite alert. That was because she had slept soundly the night before. At first, after she came here, her sleep had been fitful, as though she couldn't get used to the new surroundings, couldn't relax. Tucked into bed, her head on the pillow, she had heard and wondered about all the noises in the rooms below. The scrape of a chair being moved, the clatter of a door closing had been disturbing. Now she knew that it was the habit of General Arnold and Major Franks to sit up late, reading, conversing or studying. Sometimes General Arnold would wander out into the darkness, not returning until dawn.

"Granny might say," thought Emmeline, with a smile,

"that the General would be good company for an owl!"

This odd schedule of General Arnold's prevented Emmeline from seeing him often. Then, too, he was frequently away, over the river, at the post. Some mornings he was out before daylight, being rowed in his barge across the Hudson, coming back only at dusk. Emmeline supposed that she had not met him face-to-face in the house more than a dozen times, and then he had taken no notice of her. He seemed unaware of her presence; he scarcely spoke to Catherine Martin; he rarely addressed the two or three infantrymen who always attended him and who ate their meals in the kitchen. Morose, wrapped in his own thoughts, he seemed to Emmeline a figure of silence and mystery.

"He'll not be like that, though, when the mistress comes," Catherine Martin said. "You'll see him brighten up then! Ah, but he does adore his beautiful young wife and that baby boy of theirs! I believe he would do anything on earth to make her happy. Anything! He's twice her age, and he can never forget that she was the belle of Philadelphia, with scores of suitors courting her, and of them all she chose him."

Emmeline had asked when Mistress Arnold would arrive.

"Not until the house is quite in order. She couldn't tolerate confusion. Major Franks will go to fetch her, for it's a long journey and the General wouldn't allow her to make it without an escort."

Emmeline understood that Major Franks would leave on this errand as soon as the General's secretary should come. Colonel Richard Varick—that was the secretary's name; and though he was a young man, he was an old friend of the Arnolds'. He had been an admirer of Mistress Arnold's when she was still Peggy Shippen of Philadelphia; and he had served with the General at Saratoga. Recently Colonel Varick had been retired from the army and had gone back to studying law, which was his profession. But General Arnold had wished to have Varick with him at West Point. He would live with the family at Robinson's House; Catherine had prepared especially for him the little room which adjoined the library.

At four o'clock, Emmeline got up from her cot, combed her hair, donned a fresh cap and apron and went downstairs where Catherine was making tea. This custom Catherine regularly observed every afternoon, making it something of a rite and declaring that even in such an uncivilized place, she would behave like a civilized person. She carried the tea for General Arnold and Major Franks into the library, on the days when they were at home; her own and Emmeline's she set on the pine table beside the open door.

She said at once, that she and Emmeline were to have company today!

"It's Mr. Hugg." Catherine whisked about, smiling and exuberant. "Though neither the master nor Major Franks is in, I know they'd wish me to be hospitable to Mr. Hugg."

"But who is—"

"Sh!" Catherine's finger was at her lips. "He's in the other room, just tidying up. My sakes, if a break in the monotony isn't very nice, indeed! . . . Ah, here you are, Mr. Hugg. And this is my little helper, Emmeline Drake."

Emmeline curtsied to the man who came into the kitchen, and they sat down to their tea.

Mr. Hugg was from Philadelphia and he had brought to Robinson's House various trunks, boxes and bags of furnishings for Mistress Arnold's boudoir: the silken, down-filled comforts, the lacy pillows and silver candlesticks, the big gilt-framed mirrors and the porcelain and ivory toilet articles. There would be more to follow, Mr. Hugg said.

He was an elderly man, portly and wrinkled, with a way of puffing out his cheeks and blinking heavy-lidded eyes as he spoke in a hoarse yet not disagreeable voice. He had been employed as the Shippen family's coachman for innumerable years and had only been lent to "Miss Peggy" for this one mission. Emmeline thought he looked very much like a dignified old turtle, and his puffing and grimacing fascinated her so that she hardly listened to what he said.

By contrast, Catherine Martin fairly hung on every word that Mr. Hugg uttered. Poor Catherine! A woman born and bred to city life, she was desolate in this period of exile. As she plied him with all the delicacies of the larder, she was begging Mr. Hugg for any little anecdote or gossip of the circles she had known so well.

Mr. Hugg, when he had eaten and drunk, was most communicative. He said that people in Philadelphia seemed to think the war was going against the Americans and General Washington's army was doomed to defeat.

"Oh, no!" exclaimed Catherine and Emmeline, in a protesting duet. "It isn't—and he won't!" And Catherine added: "That would be disaster. I take no stock in such gabbling—with all due respect to you, Mr. Hugg, I'm sure."

"Well," Mr. Hugg said, "I'm telling it as I hear it, and not what I myself believe, maybe."

"You get such things from the Shippens' Loyalist friends, I daresay." Catherine bestowed a severe glance upon the visitor. "I had hoped that Mistress Arnold would have given up companions of that kind, now she's married to the General. But there, she's so young, scarce twenty; and I suppose she's in dire suspense all the while, separated from her husband."

"In suspense? Ah, that she is," said Mr. Hugg, rolling his eyes eloquently. "Why, not long ago I drove her to the home of Mr. Robert Morris, where she was invited to dine. Pretty as a picture, she was, when she stepped out of the chaise—and not an hour until I was summoned to take her back to her father's house, in as bad a spell of fainting and weeping and wailing as ever I've seen."

"You don't say!" Catherine sat on the edge of her chair. "And what caused the spell, Mr. Hugg?"

"You may well ask. I did; and it was nothing more than that another dinner guest had congratulated her on the report of General Arnold's being made commander of the army's left wing. Keeled over, she did; and wouldn't be consoled, though they insisted the commission was such a lofty and honorable one. No, ma'am! According to Miss Peggy, the General had been promised West Point, and nought else would do. She quite spoiled the dinner party. It's said the Morrises and all present were astounded at her goings-on." Mr. Hugg peered out through the door to the bedraggled lawn. "Odd, *I* think, now that I'm seeing the place."

"You should have seen it before Emmeline and I got at it, mopping and scouring."

"And that I don't doubt, ma'am. Nor do I mean the house isn't neat as wax, for it is. But Miss Peggy, she's never been one for keeping herself in out-of-the-way nooks. Not without she had a purpose, anyhow. No, to be in the midst of things, that's Miss Peggy!"

"We've been in the midst of battles," said Emmeline, "all up and down the Hudson."

"Battles? Not for Miss Peggy!" Mr. Hugg shook his head. "Perhaps she just yearns to be near the General. If so, I'm sure it's a nice sentiment and does her credit. Will you be here long, Mistress Martin?"

"I'm afraid so," Catherine said, and sighed. "I really am afraid so! Have another bit of bread, Mr. Hugg. And butter?

This is butter which the General has churned just for himself, he's that fond of it. I'll venture you've not had any truly good butter in Philadelphia since the British robbers sacked and pillaged the town. Oh, how I did dislike those redcoats! Didn't you, sir?"

"Eh?" Mr. Hugg blinked. "The British? Yes, ma'am. I did, indeed."

But he did not say it so emphatically as Emmeline could have wished. Her blue eyes bent on her plate, Emmeline decided that this Mr. Hugg might be one of those persons who, as Granny said, was neither friend nor foe but who balanced between the two classifications. Mr. Hugg was receiving a living from the Shippens, existing on the bounty of avowed Loyalists—yet also serving General Arnold, a famous patriot. How could he divide himself so, into two such different roles? Emmeline Drake could never have done it!

She was not sorry when Mr. Hugg announced that he wouldn't spend the night, but would tarry only long enough to put into the General's hands some very private papers and correspondence entrusted to him by Mistress Arnold. Then Mr. Hugg would start back immediately to Philadelphia.

9

"THE CHAIN, SIR!"

EMMELINE WAS OFTEN TO RECALL MR. HUGG'S VISIT.

Perhaps it was from this tea-time hour of an August afternoon that she dated her feeling of uncertainty about Robinson's House. Never again would things run so smoothly. Mr. Hugg seemed to have left behind him the beginnings of dissension and small, nagging arguments which were to unite finally in a stream of events as turbulent and deep as the Hudson itself. Emmeline couldn't have defined the little fear which had been planted in her heart; she was scarcely conscious of it. But afterward she could look back and know that the big white house, with its surroundings of dense forests and somber mountains, had been darkened always by grim foreshadowing.

And Emmeline, though she did her work so well, could not influence what was to happen here. She would be merely an observer of the perplexing drama.

It was the very next day after Mr. Hugg's visit that someone, at dawn, rushed up the veranda steps and pounded wildly on the front door of Robinson's House—and set up a hue and cry which was (as Catherine Martin muttered, bounding from bed and snatching at her wrapper) fit to wake the dead!

"What *is* that horrid racket?" Catherine said. "Who's calling so early?"

Running downstairs behind Catherine, clutching the skirts of her own wrapper, her braids bouncing on her shoulders, Emmeline recognized the caller who impetuously pushed his way into the hall.

"Why, it's Mr. Rawlins," Emmeline thought. "Jed knows him. He sometimes passes our cottage and exchanges a few civil words with Granny."

But what had brought Mr. Rawlins to this place before sunup?

He was asking breathlessly for General Arnold. "Quick!" he urged. "Quick! I've got to see him!"

Catherine hesitated only an instant. Then she darted toward the General's door and knocked. There was a brief silence, a trickle of smothered exclamations, and the General appeared.

He had thrown a black silk dressing-gown around him and he came stamping down the hall in leather slippers. His face was still ruddy from sleep, but his eyes were keen as a hawk's. He looked every inch the brilliant, able soldier, ready to command. Behind him Major Franks trotted, struggling to button his military blouse and seem calm and efficient.

"Well?" General Arnold said. "What is it?"

Rawlins twisted his cap in gnarled, work-worn hands. His hair was tousled over his forehead and his immense boots were muddying Catherine's clean floor. He started to speak, rather incoherently, in great agitation.

"The chain, sir! Oh, I wouldn't 'a' believed it! No, sir! But there I was, seeing the water and the eddying current. Something was different, and I knew it!"

"Different?" repeated the General.

"With the chain, sir."

"What chain?"

"Why, in the river! The chain to hold the Britishers off. I saw it was different—and *wrong*. I steered alongside and I reached my arm down—see how wet I am, sir?—and I grabbed at the chain. I said to myself that it couldn't be cut, for whatever would be sharp enough to bite through those giant links? But then, slipping and slipping my hand along, I came to the loose end. *Loose,* sir! One link was open, so that the next would pull through as the current pressed against it. I knew there was nothing *I* could do, with a single link so weighty that one man couldn't budge it—so I paddled for the bank, fast as I could, to tell you!"

Emmeline's eyes were upon Rawlins and she understood just how he felt, his consternation and panic. To people in the Highlands, the chain in the Hudson seemed a guaranty of security. While it was whole and intact, no enemy ships could approach. To think of its being damaged was terrifying. She waited for General Arnold's reply. Would he be amazed and angry?

He was cool, staring at Rawlins. "Who are you?"

Rawlins looked blank. "A fisherman, sir. Every morning I put out from Buttermilk Falls. Today I was taking my boat across stream—well, it's not my boat, but my cousin's, for mine was reefed last week. But, anyway, I noticed how the water was, all furrowed in eddies, as if with a log stuck in the channel. So I reached my arm down—"

"And your arm is wet. Yes, you've said that. What is your name?"

"John Rawlins." The man shifted his muddy boots. He spied Emmeline in the background and his face lightened. "There's the Drake girl. She knows me."

"Oh, yes!" Emmeline said impulsively. "I—"

The General turned and stared at Emmeline as if he were seeing her for the first time; and she blushed and said nothing more. Then the General turned again to Rawlins. "You are trying to tell me that the chain across the Hudson has been tampered with?"

"Yes, sir. Broken—or cut."

"Incredible!"

"But, sir, it is!"

"I myself examined the links only yesterday. Each one was sound as a nut."

Rawlins seemed crestfallen. "Maybe in the night, somebody was prying at it—"

"Somebody?"

"Some traitor, sir, who would destroy it."

"You let your fancy deceive you, my good fellow."

"No, sir. I'm not fancying anything."

"There are no traitors at West Point," said the General, "or on Martalaer's Rock—or here." His eyes glinted. "As for Buttermilk Falls, I'm not so sure. If the chain is loosened, it may be because of your meddling."

"*Mine?*" Rawlins flushed brick-red.

"Perhaps that's what is wrong, and your coming like this is a ruse to avert suspicion from yourself."

"Sir," Rawlins said simply. "I am a patriot."

"Are you, indeed? But not in the army, not fighting for your country."

"I *was* in the army. Ten months—and wounded."

Very abruptly, as if the subject bored him, General Arnold shrugged and made a gesture of dismissal. To Major Franks he said: "You will see to this nonsense, please."

"Yes, sir." Major Franks was rather pale, the scar on his jaw showed distinctly.

"Investigate the fantastic tale—I have no faith in it—and do what you think is necessary. But mark you!" He swung about to glare at the miserable, outraged Rawlins. "Mark you, if there's treachery *anywhere*, even in Buttermilk Falls, it will be punished. I'm going back to bed, Franks; I'll expect your report at breakfast."

"Yes, sir."

General Arnold swept his silk robe closer around him and strode out of sight.

"Come, Rawlins." Major Franks' voice was gentle as he touched the fisherman's dripping sleeve. "You must go with me to investigate."

"I will. And thank you, sir," said Rawlins humbly.

"So, Franks, that abominably dirty fellow was not lying?"

"He was not lying, sir."

General Arnold sat back in his chair at the breakfast table and puffed at his long-stemmed clay pipe. "The chain has been fooled with, eh?"

A dish in each of her hands, Emmeline paused in the pantry door to hear the Major's answer. If this was eavesdropping, Emmeline did not care. All her young sympathy had gone out to John Rawlins, who in that morning scene had been so earnest, so pitiably mistaken. She would have sworn to Rawlins' patriotism—and she had hated the General's haughty disbelief, his air of patronage. She had thought of another morning, at the Haverstraw tavern and Kirby shrinking away from a slapping glove. She knew now that her first glimpse of a famous man had not misled her. This was the real Benedict Arnold, whatever else he might seem to other people.

Major Franks was kindling his own pipe. "The chain has been loosened," he said.

General Arnold struck his fist on the table. "Who could have done it? What person in New York is so dastardly? I knew, of course, that we had enemies about us—"

"Plenty of them, sir. And traitors. An out-and-out enemy is not so dangerous to my mind as a cowardly traitor."

"You are right, Franks. We must be on our guard. And

yet—can you think of no other explanation than treachery?"

Major Franks said slowly that the links might have been imperfectly forged and then loosened by natural causes.

"The force of the current? It's very strong at that point, eh?" The smoke from General Arnold's pipe curved in a graceful blue wisp. "I shall hope that it *was* a natural cause."

"That the current and not a person was the culprit?"

"Yes. And if the occasion arises, I shall say as much. Accidental damage. You would not contradict me, Franks?"

"I could not contradict you, sir," the Major said.

"After all, we've had no strangers here. Just ourselves."

"And Mr. Hugg."

"Hugg?" The General laughed. "That honest old fogy? You mustn't joke about this, Franks."

"I'm not joking. You mentioned strangers. Mr. Hugg is a stranger."

"Not to me. Hugg, indeed! Imagine him diving into the Hudson and grappling with cold iron! Why, you couldn't get him into a bathtub without a team of horses! I must tell Peggy about your suggesting Hugg as our culprit. She will be highly amused. Poor, comical old Hugg." General Arnold waved his pipe. "Well, to be serious, Franks—it's fortunate we found out about the chain in time to mend it."

"Fortunate," said the Major, even more slowly, "that Rawlins found out."

"Yes. Rawlins." General Arnold nodded. "You thought I was short with him, did you?"

"You seemed rather short, sir."

"If so, I am sorry. Sincerely sorry. But he was very *wet;* and perhaps I'm not at my best before dawn. Well, I'll make it up to Rawlins. Yes, I'll give Rawlins a bottle of wine. You can take it to him, Franks. Or Varick can take it. He comes today, you know. I could send the gift by a trooper, but Rawlins would be pleased to have an officer asking for him in Buttermilk Falls. Set him up, you know. He'll feel like a hero before the villagers. Yes, you must be my messenger to Rawlins, my dove of peace. Or Varick. You and Varick can toss a coin for it."

Major Franks was silent.

Emmeline went into the kitchen where Catherine was kneading a batch of dough. *"I,"* said Emmeline, "would fling that bottle of wine smack into the Hudson!"

"What's that?" Catherine glanced up. "What bottle? What are you chattering about, child?"

"Nothing. Catherine, did you know that Colonel Varick is coming today?"

"Is he? That's nice. Colonel Varick is an amiable young gentleman. I'll be glad to have him."

Emmeline fidgeted. There was something she wanted to say. Presently she burst out: "Catherine, I've always thought a servant must *admire* his master or mistress, that a servant ought not work for someone he couldn't really admire."

Catherine pommeled the bulging dough, her arms very pink and muscular. "Don't talk so fast, Emmeline. Now what—"

"I'm saying that a servant really should like the person he serves."

"Well, it's better that way. Much better. What servant are you speaking of, and what master?"

"Oh, none in particular." Emmeline clattered the dishes into a pan and reached for the soap. "Only I'm not very experienced as a pantry-maid."

"No, you're not. But you're learning." Catherine smiled and the butterfly bow on her brown hair bobbed cheerfully. "Does anything trouble you?"

"I was thinking that perhaps if a servant—a pantry-maid, for instance—realizes suddenly that she simply can't admire her employer, she should—well, quit."

Catherine seemed to consider this idea. "No, I think not, Emmeline. Unless the employer has some bad fault. I mean *bad,* like stealing or being cruel, or something *sinful.* There's a gap between the little, annoying things and the big ones, the bad ones."

"Yes," Emmeline said. "I suppose so."

"Work is hard to get and wages very nice to have. Of course, *I* must work."

"And I must, too." Emmeline wondered if Catherine guessed what was in her mind.

"I've been with the Arnolds a long time. They often rile me with their little ways and peculiarities. But everyone is peculiar."

"You're not. I'm not."

"We may be. Yes, I think we are. And I never, never doubt that the Arnolds are honorable, Emmeline. You mustn't doubt it, either." Catherine tapped with a floury finger on Emmeline's shoulder. "Now you go out with your basket and gather some ripe, red apples from the tree in the yard. I'll bake a tart for supper. As I remember, Colonel Varick just dotes on apple tart."

10

AN AMIABLE YOUNG GENTLEMAN

EMMELINE'S FIRST VIEW OF COLONEL RICHARD VARICK WAS from above, for she was still in the apple tree, balanced among the boughs, the basket hooked over her arm, one hand holding her skirts, the other outstretched, when a procession of three figures straggled up the path from Beverley Dock. She thought the man in front must be General Arnold's secretary; the other two were porters, loaded with luggage. Each porter had a trunk on his shoulders and they were sweating, as if the trunks were heavy. Colonel Varick himself was not unencumbered; he carried a hamper, a parcel and a shabby violin case.

As the procession reached the house, Emmeline saw Catherine Martin run out, followed by Major Franks, who cried: "Welcome! Welcome!" Then some soldiers appeared, to help the porters with the trunks. Everyone went inside, and Emmeline descended from the tree.

She wondered what on earth Colonel Varick had in his luggage.

"Books," Catherine said. "If he weren't an army officer, Colonel Varick would be a bookworm." She smiled, and added: "You'll soon see I'm right."

Yes, Colonel Varick had brought books to Robinson's House, dozens and scores of them; and Emmeline was told to help him stack them in his room. She went to the door and curtsied.

"Catherine Martin said—"

A procession of three figures straggled up the path

"Come in, whoever you are."

"I'm Emmeline."

"Well, Emmeline," Colonel Varick said, "I need assistance."

As they worked together, filling every available space with books, Emmeline glanced shyly at the newcomer. In looks, he was more the student than the soldier, tall and thin, rather stooped, and his uniform fit him none too well. His hair was the color of sand, his light brown eyes were bright. His complexion proved that he had not recently been exposed to sun and wind; and Emmeline remembered what Catherine Martin had said—that after an army career, Colonel Varick had retired to read law with his father. He was returning now to military duty at General Arnold's special request; but the law would, perhaps, always be his main profession.

Colonel Varick had, in fact, thought to continue his studies in the Highlands; he hadn't anticipated that to be a secretary was such arduous work and he was, therefore, somewhat surprised to find his desk heaped with papers and documents and the General's correspondence.

"You mean," he said to Major Franks, who strolled in to watch the unpacking, "I must busy myself *immediately?*"

"Those are orders—with the General's compliments."

"Very good, Franks. I have the capacity for diligence, I am not a shirker. And Emmeline here will finish the stacking." Grinning ruefully at the Major, Colonel Varick took quill pen and ink and went at the papers.

In the evening of that day—and every evening thereafter, he played the violin, stepping out upon the veranda when the summer darkness had fallen, lounging against a pillar, playing and playing, melancholy and sentimental tunes.

As a musician he had some skill. Back in the kitchen,

Catherine and Emmeline would listen and nod their heads in time with the melody. Emmeline loved music and the sound of it was somehow reassuring in this sequestered spot—but she did wish that Colonel Varick would not incline so much to the mournful!

"If only he'd play *Yankee Doodle,* Catherine!"

"Ah, there's a song!" Then Catherine, who had known the colonel for so long and who had made him an apple tart, would call out: "If you please, Mr. Richard, we'd like *Yankee Doodle.*"

And obligingly Colonel Varick would scrape the boisterous strains of that from his violin—before drifting off again into ballads of love and longing.

"He was one of the many suitors Miss Peggy Shippen rejected for General Arnold," said Catherine.

"Of the two, I should have taken Colonel Varick," said Emmeline. "And I'd think he wouldn't want to be here, now that she is Mistress Arnold."

"Oh, he's the romantic sort," said Catherine. "He's really *quite* young and enjoys picturing himself as suffering. As for that, every man who sees Miss Peggy is her adorer."

"*I* am eager to see her," said Emmeline.

Colonel Varick and Major Franks were friends of several years. Frequently they sat together, an hour or more, over their pipes. But as the General's aide, Major Franks had to spend the main part of each day at West Point—where Colonel Varick was seldom permitted to go.

"Franks," the Colonel said, "I'm tied to this desk! I had no notion there'd be such a prodigious lot of writing to do. Why, the General is making lists—of *everything.* Tabulating the number of men in his command, classifying them as gunners, sharpshooters, foragers, or whatnot; tabulating the cannon, the powder, the ball; noting the amounts of supplies, flour, salt, sugar, fats. He has counted the horses and mules. By George, he seems almost to have counted the cats and rats that roam about the camp. And all these items of information I must copy and recopy—and then do it all again!"

"He is conscientious and precise," said Major Franks. "He wants to be able to say to General Washington that he has been systematic in the conduct of the post."

"Yes, I know. But I should like occasionally to vary the program. Robinson's House may get on my nerves."

Major Franks laughed. "Oh, I daresay you'll be more content when Mistress Arnold arrives. I am to go soon to Philadelphia to escort the lady."

"You are fortunate," said Colonel Varick, smiling.

Major Franks told his friend about his own duties. He was often detailed to Fort Putnam up in the hills. He described this fortress, which had been so cleverly built of rocks and earth that it seemed to be a part of the steep bluffs and, at a distance, scarcely could be distinguished for what it was, a sod-roofed structure concealing brick-walled cells, like rabbit warrens, tunneling underground. In these cells were benches, bunks, fireplaces and racks for weapons. The doors were thick panels of oak, iron-barred; once the doors were shut, it would be difficult, indeed, to dislodge the defenders of Fort Putnam.

Major Franks described also the works at West Point. He was a man of true military tastes and could become enthusiastic in discussing war and its devices.

"To appreciate West Point, you should see a plan of it, Varick."

"I have seen one."

"What?" Major Franks arched his brows in astonishment.

"And a plan of Putnam, Webb, Wyllys, Montgomery, Clinton. General Arnold has copies of them all."

"I hope they're kept under lock and key."

"In my desk, Franks." The Colonel paused. "Why do you say that?"

"Well, there might be a spy about. Who knows?" Major Franks lowered his voice. "You've heard the chain was unlinked?"

"In the Hudson? Yes. You believe that was done purposely?"

"It—it would seem so, Varick."

"And you suspect someone?"

"No. But the country is riddled with Loyalists—and the country folk come and go, bringing food, poultry and vegetables, for the table here."

"The General doesn't seem suspicious."

"Perhaps not suspicious enough," said Major Franks.

"It's possible." Varick mused. "This Mr. Joshua Hett Smith to whom the General often writes—is he a Loyalist?"

"He has been accused of it."

"Ah? And you think—"

"No," the Major said, "I think, more likely, Smith is one of those men who are acting as agents, and General Arnold uses him as a counter-spy to procure information from British agents. Since it isn't known just who or what he is, Smith can wander at will—and into many regions from which an identified patriot would be excluded."

"Spies and counter-spies? I don't like the system, Franks."

"Nor do I. And yet it's common with both armies. Almost every commander, American and British, has his staff of secret agents."

"If Smith should be really a Loyalist, General Arnold might become badly involved and criticized. Why don't you warn him to proceed cautiously with this Mr. Smith?"

"I have thought of doing so," said Major Franks. "But, after all, I am only a subordinate here. You outrank me, Varick. Why don't *you* warn him?"

"Perhaps I will," said the Colonel, "for I am devoted to him; and I feel that, with all that has happened to him in the past, he must be exceedingly careful of his reputation."

As the days went by, Colonel Varick seemed always to be busier; and Emmeline would see him casting longing glances at his books, as if he would have preferred poring over them rather than sitting endlessly at his desk. He was courteous to Emmeline and questioned her as to her family and how she had come into service at Robinson's House. She told him about Jed, and the Colonel was interested.

"I should like to meet your brother," he said.

It was Emmeline who first gave Colonel Varick the news of the woodcutters' departure from West Point. She had walked down to the dock that morning, and the sight of several large boats on the river had made her curious. When she returned to the house she mentioned the circumstance to the Colonel.

"Boats? What kind of boats, Emmeline? Where from?"

"I think they put out from the fort, sir."

In haste, Colonel Varick went to the dock. Three soldiers were there, painting and caulking General Arnold's barge which was moored at the pier. The soldiers said yes, they also had seen the boats, but they did not know who the passengers were.

In the late afternoon, Major Franks, back from drill, told Colonel Varick that the boats had contained two hundred woodcutters sent out by General Arnold on an excursion to obtain a winter's supply of fuel for the West Point garrison.

Varick was perturbed. "Two hundred men! What an absurd thing to do! This is no time to be weakening our forces—every breeze that blows bears the rumor of a British attack!"

"The General said we need wood."

"We need arms much more, Franks. If Sir Henry Clinton struck us suddenly, we'd never need the wood at all!"

"Why don't you tell the General that?"

"I will. Tonight, at supper. By George, I'll—I'll *remonstrate*."

"Then I'll not sup with you. I shall beg to be excused. Your remonstrating would be painful for me to witness, and embarrassing for the General."

"Do as you wish, Franks. But I'll speak to him."

But that night, at the meal from which Major Franks had so tactfully absented himself, it was General Arnold who spoke first. He said that a certain lady, from a town above West Point, had asked him for a "flag" which would take her and her small children through the American lines to join her husband in New York City. Such a "flag" was not a banner of any sort, but a letter signed by the General. As secretary, Colonel Varick had written several passes, or "flags," for no traveler could go unchallenged down the Hudson.

"Is the lady a Loyalist, sir?"

"Yes, Varick. She is a Loyalist."

The Colonel laid down his fork. "Then I am very much opposed to writing her a flag."

"You are? And why?"

"I think it's most inadvisable, sir. In the short while I've been with you, I've noted how liberal you are with these letters. Loyalists, or persons thought to be Loyalists, are constantly wanting passes to go here and there, and you grant them. I'm fearful of the consequences. Not for myself—for you."

"But I am discreet in deciding which persons deserve the flags. You say I'm liberal. Perhaps. But no evil has come of it."

"Not yet. No, sir."

General Arnold looked at his secretary and seemed to ponder. In the glow of the candles, his handsome, swarthy countenance was warm and smiling. He had removed his coat and donned the fine silk dressing-gown he so often wore. His collar and ruffled shirt-front were snowy white, and he had looped up his queue with a velvet ribbon.

"You do guard me, don't you, Varick?"

"I wish to, sir."

"Against the day of reckoning? Pshaw! This lady is a friend of Peggy's."

"A Loyalist friend of Mistress Arnold's?"

"A *former* friend, I should have said."

"And she is going to New York?"

"Her husband is in the city."

"It means, doesn't it, that the husband has made his peace with the British? Otherwise, he wouldn't be tolerated there. Perhaps the husband would be glad to have information of our regiments in the Highlands."

"Information?"

"There have been women spies in history."

As Arnold only shook his head, Colonel Varick went on: "I had thought to speak to you on another matter this evening. Your dispatching of the woodcutters—was that judicious, sir? You take two hundred men from the fort and thereby you greatly weaken it. Is this strategy? Would General Washington sanction it, sir?"

"Of course, I shall report without delay to General Washington."

"I think His Excellency will doubt your good judgment—as I do, sir."

General Arnold kept his eyes, so black and intent, upon Varick, and he was still smiling. "You are an impudent young wretch," he said, but without a trace of anger in his

AN AMIABLE YOUNG GENTLEMAN 97

tone. "I would chastise you—except that I know you are as jealous of my honor as I am, myself. Well, Colonel, you may be right. It may be that I should not have sent out the woodcutters." He leaned elbows on the table. "Let me make a bargain with you. I will recall them tomorrow—and you, without further protest, withdraw your objections to the issuing of a flag for the lady, who is most surely as innocent and blameless as a lamb. What do you say, Varick?"

"Well, sir, since you trust the lady—"

"I do. There is no reason why I shouldn't be frank with you, Varick. In New York City is a man named John Anderson—or so he calls himself. He has the opportunity to be very valuable to me. He says he can establish a line of intelligence to the enemy's movements, and I believe him."

"John Anderson? A secret agent?"

"Yes, I suppose he is that. We have communicated, Anderson and I, our messages cloaked in a mercantile style of writing."

"In code, sir?"

"Exactly. In code. It is a proper correspondence which is consistent with the discharge of my duty. It will be commendable if I get this intelligence from Anderson—as I expect to. Do you grant as much, Colonel?"

"I could not deny it, sir."

"Very well. Now, this lady, Mistress Mary McCarthy, is to be the emissary who bears a letter to Anderson. I have already spoken to Colonel Sheldon, who commands at Lower Salem, south of here. I desire Mistress McCarthy to have a pass and an escort. I am so sure of her that I will write the flag myself, in my own hand; and thus you will not incur any risk." General Arnold paused. "Does that satisfy you, Colonel?"

"You are my superior officer, sir."

"Yes, and an officer mindful of all hazards, at all times. I have endured much injustice, Varick. I have been discriminated against and persecuted. I have seen men far less talented than I elevated to positions which should have been mine. I have coped with stubborn prejudice and struggled against scornful publicity. But I have been indomitable. I have risen above the petty snarling of envious politicians. I have triumphed—and I shall go on triumphing. Be faithful to me, my boy, and you will be rewarded beyond your dreams!"

"I am faithful to you, sir," said Varick quietly. "I want no other reward than your success, and my country's freedom."

11

KIRBY'S INSPIRATION

WHISTLING AND IN THE BEST OF SPIRITS, KIRBY DRAKE STROLLED toward Haverstraw through morning sunshine. Under his arm was a bulky package—Mr. Joshua Smith's fine coat, which at last Granny had finished and which Kirby would deliver to its owner. Kirby was glad to be going to Mr. Smith's house, for he had private business in the vicinity. On the Smith estate were two tenants, Samuel and Joseph Cahoon, and Kirby had been dickering with one of these men.

Samuel Cahoon had said he might purchase a young pig—might even buy five pigs! The prospect excited Kirby. He had learned recently that there were plenty of people about who wanted little pigs; but few—alas!—who could pay in coin for them. A trade was not to be considered, for what could Kirby have done with the things offered him in trade? A plough, a rake, a hoe, a potful of flaxseed, a gallon jug of syrup—they were all very nice to have, of course; but none would have been of the slightest help in getting Granny launched on the journey to Rhode Island.

Kirby felt quite reconciled now to selling Patience's babies, he could think of it without more than a shadow of regret. They were growing up at an astonishing rate; they were not beautiful; they seemed all to have inherited their mother's difficult disposition and lack of manners; they had the habit of being terribly naughty; and they were simply the hungriest animals Kirby had ever seen. When one day the pigs broke out of the shed and rooted up Granny's garden, and the very next day scampered off into the potato patch of a neighbor, and there gorged themselves on stolen food, Kirby knew that to keep them would mean not only that the Drakes might be eaten out of house and home, but also that he was likely to become a most unpopular person in the countryside.

He was now discovering that the sacrifice he had been asked to make would not, after all, be such a dreadful one. Indeed, the sacrifice, once he faced it, seemed unimportant.

"Perhaps," he thought, "that often happens and probably somebody has invented a maxim about it—something like 'Don't borrow trouble,' or 'Cows at a distance have long horns.' I daresay Granny could tell me, or Emmeline; they're always quoting maxims."

He realized also that his idea of a pig farm was not very practical either—not with pigs such nuisances! But he knew quite well that he would insist upon staying in the cottage during the winter while Granny and the others of the family were away. He would be a hermit! It would be great fun to be alone, and never have to mind anybody, or wash, or go to bed until he was good and ready, or study his primer or Bible lessons; and he was sure he could find many interesting things to do.

When he reached the lane that verged toward Mr. Smith's house, Kirby could tell by the sun that the hour must be close upon nine, yet as he approached the big square stone mansion, he saw no signs of activity. The windows were shuttered, the veranda was deserted. He feared that no one was at home—and what would he do with the package then? But when he went around to the rear and knocked, the door of the summer kitchen was opened by a woman whom he recognized as the housekeeper.

"For Mr. Smith," said Kirby, holding out the package, "from Mistress Drake of near Donderberg."

"Oh, yes. His coat, eh?"

"His coat."

"Mr. Smith is still abed," said the woman. "He has some guests and they sat late, eating and drinking. I'm not to disturb them until noon. Will you tell Mistress Drake that when the master rides out today, he will stop and settle his account with her?"

Kirby nodded. Mr. Smith's credit was good.

"Maybe you'd like to come in for a wafer and a mug of ale?"

"A mug of *milk* would be refreshing," said Kirby. "And thank you very kindly, ma'am."

He perched on a stool while the woman fetched the milk. This kitchen was large, with so many brightly burnished utensils on the hearth that Kirby was struck with wonder.

"How much cooking you must do here! Is the family a big one?"

"No," said the woman. "Just the master and the mistress and their nephew who makes his home with them. At present Mistress Smith and the lad are away. But Mr. Smith often has company, as he did last night." She peeped into the oven. "Would you like this bit of roast fowl? It is a leftover."

"Thank you, ma'am." Kirby nibbled at the chicken wing which was crisply brown and tasty. "I daresay you are famous for your cooking."

"Oh, well, I don't know that I am." Smilingly, she added: "Though people do tell me so, it's true. General Arnold now, he vows he's always happy to be invited to this house, knowing the food will be delicious. It rather puts me on my mettle, such a pretty speech. I am thinking of some treat for his breakfast today."

"General Benedict Arnold? Is he one of the company?"

"Yes. He arrived yesterday and spent the night; he and the master were joined by friends. The meal I fixed for them was almost a banquet—if I do say so, that shouldn't! Maybe you noticed the General's barge down by the river's edge?"

"I did not come that way, but by the road."

"Do you know the General?"

"Not really. I have seen him."

Kirby had eaten the wafer, drunk the milk and gnawed the chicken wing to the bone. He slipped down from the stool, bowed politely and said that he must be off to seek the Cahoon brothers.

"The Cahoons? But they are not here this morning."

"Not Mr. Samuel Cahoon?"

"Neither of them," said the woman. "They drove to Tappan just after daybreak and will not be back until tomorrow."

This was more of a disappointment than Kirby cared to admit. He had been counting on completing the transaction with Mr. Samuel. Now he would have to go home, his business indefinitely postponed and with a sense of anticlimax.

Of course, he said nothing of his feelings to Mr. Smith's housekeeper. Instead he went out of the summer kitchen and sauntered idly across the yard and down to the river, to have a look at General Arnold's barge.

It was riding at anchor on the yellow water beside Mr. Smith's pier—a long, low flatboat so big that it carried four sets of rowlocks and would accommodate several passengers under the queer, oblong-shaped canopy of canvas erected as a screen for rain or sun. Behind the canopy and the seats it sheltered was a skiff raised on the deck, battened down and shrouded with a burlap cover. Eight brawny men were lying in the grass on the river bank, their hats tilted over their faces. Apparently these were General Arnold's oarsmen—and they were fast asleep, for the shuffle of Kirby's feet on the shale did not rouse them.

Kirby looked at the barge. It made him think of Emmeline. He often thought of her, and missed her. Indeed, he wouldn't have had anyone on earth know how lonely he had been for his sister, during the several weeks that she had been away. He did wish that he could see Emmeline. Now all of August had passed and nine days of September—and no sight of Emmeline, only a letter occasionally, when she could get someone to take a letter over the river to Buttermilk Falls or the inn at Haverstraw. He supposed Emmeline must be missing him, too . . .

It was then, suddenly, that Kirby had his marvelous inspiration. He crept out on the pier and dropped over the side; he crept to the end of the barge, uncovered the skiff and crawled in. Glancing back, he saw that the oarsmen were still soundly sleeping. He pulled the burlap over the skiff, leaving a little space for breathing purposes. Then he lay flat on the bottom of the skiff.

He was very warm and cozy under his burlap roof. The barge rocked gently with the swaying of the small waves.

"Ho-hum!" yawned Kirby, and soon he was sunk in slumber.

It was late afternoon when he awakened; Kirby could tell as much by the slanting of shadows on the brown cloth above him. He could hear the brisk creak of the oars and the swish of water and knew that the barge must be moving upstream at a rapid speed. He lifted himself enough to peep out through the space in the cover. Under the canopy, within Kirby's range of vision, a man was sitting—General Arnold, very splendid in white breeches and blue cloak. The General had a pad on his knee; he was writing, pausing now and then to gaze off into the distance. Behind him three gentlemen in civilian dress were dozing in their chairs, their heads lolled back and mouths gaping.

Kirby lay down again in the skiff, and hoped that dusk would fall before the voyage had ended. Somehow, his inspiration of being a stowaway seemed less attractive, with the General so close at hand. He tried to imagine how he would get out of his hiding-place without being detected, once the barge had docked. He had no difficulty at all in imagining what the General might say or do if the unbidden passenger were caught.

But, as a matter of fact, the disembarking was almost ridiculously easy. When at twilight the barge snubbed into the Beverley Dock, General Arnold and the three gentlemen were already on their feet and stepping out upon the boards, their voices quickly fading to a murmur and lost among the trees. The oarsmen tied up the boat with stout ropes and prepared to follow.

There was just an instant of apprehension—when one oarsman called out: "Shall I look in the skiff for luggage to be hauled ashore?" But his mates replied: "No, the General had nought this trip. Hurry along, Ben. Mistress Martin'll be dishing up the victuals."

Kirby waited until the men, too, had gone. Then he got out, stretched himself, jumped to the ground and started up the path between the overhanging willows.

It was dark as he came in view of many windows shedding candle light. He walked gingerly from one window to the next, anxious for a glimpse of Emmeline. He did not see her. He had thought she would be in the pantry (wasn't she a pantry-maid?) but the only person there was a stocky woman with a white bow, like a butterfly, in her hair.

Kirby began to be afraid he had made some absurd error. Could it possibly be that this wasn't Robinson's House at all, that he was mistaken in his destination? He started a second circuit of the windows, and saw a short flight of stairs leading down into an areaway. On impulse he went down, and through an open door.

He was in a cellar which had a corridor lined with doors. He walked, gropingly, the length of the corridor, turned and retraced his steps. On the floor was a patch of white. He bent and picked up a crumpled sheet of paper which he stuffed into his pocket. He stopped.

Someone was descending from the outside. Against the gray rectangle of the entrance, a man's figure was silhouetted, tall and thin, with stooping shoulders. The man came toward Kirby, slowly, trying all the corridor doors. Kirby crouched against the wall.

And then he sneezed.

The man ran forward and grabbed him by the arm, pulled him into the areaway and up the stairs, through the grass and around the house and inside. Then Kirby was standing, blinking, in a brightly lighted room, being stared at by the tall, thin man and the woman with the bow in her hair.

"Observe, Catherine, what I found in the basement."

"Well, I never!"

"You know the lad?"

"Never laid eyes on him in my life, Mr. Richard."

"Is he one of our prowling Loyalist cowboys up to deviltry?"

"I wouldn't doubt it, sir, for he's surely too small and young to be a proper spy. He says nothing. P'rhaps the cat's got his tongue."

"Ought I hand him over to General Arnold?"

"I think so, Mr. Richard."

Kirby had been too terrified to say anything, or to struggle to free himself. But now he said loudly: "Let me go! No, I'm not a cowboy or a spy. Yes, I was down there, but I intended no deviltry. I'm looking for my sister."

"Your sister?" The woman shook her head. "A likely tale!"

"As for that," said Kirby, growing bolder, "what were *you* doing, sir, trying all the doors?"

He was somewhat surprised at the abrupt silence his question caused. The woman seemed almost to forget about him; she looked at the man she had called "Mr. Richard"; and the man's eyes shifted and he laughed, rather self-consciously.

And just at that moment skirts swished and a girl came into the room.

"Why—why, Kirby!" said Emmeline. "Is it *you?*"

"It's me," squeaked Kirby, miserably.

12

STOWAWAY'S FLIGHT

WHAT WITH THE EXCLAMATIONS OF EMMELINE, AND KIRBY'S attempts to tell where he'd come from, the ensuing few minutes were extremely flurried; but Kirby knew, with relief, that both "Mr. Richard" and the woman were more friendly than they had seemed. As if amused, they smiled at Emmeline and her brother; and the tall, thin man said he wouldn't report the informal arrival.

"Nor will I," said Catherine Martin. "What the General don't know can't hurt him. I do declare, though, you've run in upon us at a bad time for visiting. Here's a houseful of guests, and me with nothing fancy to feed them! Your sister and I can't twiddle our thumbs and gossip with you —not until we have the meal on the table. Well, Master Kirby—if that's your name—you make yourself small there in the corner. Keep out from under our feet, and presently I'll fix you some supper."

Obediently Kirby took up a post in the corner behind the oven. He was very cheerful and watched with interest the gathering together of what he considered a tremendous quantity of the most excellent and appetizing food.

Sometimes Emmeline would throw a sentence to him, as if he were a robin to be tossed a crumb.

"That was Colonel Varick, Kirby; the General's secretary . . . We always have soldiers about, but not so many now as usually. Major Franks, the General's aide, has gone to Philadelphia to bring back Mistress Arnold and the baby . . . You needn't be frightened, for the General seldom comes into this part of the house; and, anyway, he's up in his chamber, changing his clothes . . . See, Kirby, the gentlemen are to have wine and they'll be merry over it!"

Kirby himself scarcely ventured a syllable for more than two hours. Then, with Emmeline on one side of him and Catherine at the other, and large plates of supper before them all, he related the happenings of the day and especially of his stolen passage up the Hudson.

"I thought it was a good chance to see you, Emmy; and the only chance I'd have for months."

"There, there," said Catherine Martin, beaming sympathetically, "I wish *I* had such a loving brother."

"Yes, but what will Granny be thinking? Won't she worry?"

"Not much, for I told her I might stay overnight with the Cahoons. I'm going to sell the pigs to Mr. Samuel Cahoon, Emmy—at least, I hope so! Granny knows about it; she says I'm to buy shoes with the money." Kirby chuckled. "Hermits don't wear shoes; they walk barefoot all the year 'round."

"You're not a hermit."

"Not yet, no."

Emmeline was meditating. "But how will you get home again? Have you thought of that?"

No. Kirby had not thought of that at all, and was not inclined to fret. If worst came to worst, he supposed he could swim. He was a good swimmer.

"Oh, Kirby, dear!"

Catherine had a suggestion. The General was going down the river again tomorrow; she'd heard the bargemen saying so when she gave them their evening's rations.

"Since the boy came on the barge, why shouldn't he

leave on it, and alight at Smith's dock, right where he started from?"

"Hiding in the skiff? Isn't that too dangerous?"

"Not for quick-witted Master Kirby! Now," Catherine said, "let's not spoil his pleasure, Emmeline. I'll spread a pallet for him in the barn, a pillow, quilt, everything; I'll wake him at dawn, and he can streak down to the river while General Arnold is drinking his morning cup. If he's in the skiff, as he was today, who'll be the wiser? Or maybe you'd rather get the General's permission?"

"No!" said Kirby vehemently.

And Emmeline echoed: "No. No, Catherine, your idea is better."

After that, for a long time after, they chatted, until the candles guttered and the logs on the hearth were nothing more than ragged and feathery pink ashes. Kirby's eyes felt heavy; he leaned against Emmeline. Her voice and Catherine's seemed to dwindle and blur . . .

"Ah, but what *was* Mr. Richard doing? I'd like to know, Emmeline. It's not the first night, either. Last week, when the master was at the fort, Colonel Varick was below there."

"In the cellar?"

"Yes. I went down—and how addled he was! 'Well,' I said, 'did you want something, sir?' And he quizzed me about the keys."

"The keys?"

"I have them. To every door in the house—except that one. General Arnold gave them to me the day we took possession. And I'll keep them and never lend them, not even to Mr. Richard, though he is such an amiable young gentleman. I don't believe the General would want to have his secretary so curious about that storeroom. I've a mind to tell the General. But no, perhaps I won't."

"You mean the General has a storeroom down there?"

"And no one ever goes into it but himself. Yes, that's what I mean. And why not? It's his own house."

"But what's in the room, Catherine?"

"How in creation would I know? His belongings and treasures."

"Maybe," said Emmeline, "that's why he goes down into the cellar so often at night. I've heard him. It will be late, when we're all in bed. Sometimes a soldier is with him, or two soldiers, or several. The men come by the river path and they have boxes. The General steps out, meets them, then they all tramp down the areaway stair."

"Emmeline!" Catherine cried. "What are you saying?"

"It's quite true."

"But I've known nothing of it. Nothing!"

"Well, I have."

"I can't think there are any such goings-on in this house! You must be dreaming—like this boy."

"No," Emmeline said. "Not dreaming. But Kirby—"

"He's more than half asleep. I'll make his pallet."

"Thank you, Catherine. And I'll help him across the yard and into the barn. Poor, tired Kirby. Dear Kirby."

In that vague moment in the barn, while Emmy was taking off his jacket and easing his belt, Kirby roused sufficiently to remember something.

"The bit of paper in my pocket, Emmy. I picked it up from the cellar floor; I don't know why. I think maybe it's a letter."

"Yes, it is." By the flicker of candle flame she scrutinized the paper. "Signed 'Gustavus.' But the language is strange, and there's no 'Gustavus' here. Well, I shall try to find the writer. Good night, Kirby."

Somehow, Kirby's return voyage was quite devoid of

"Sometimes a soldier is with him and they have boxes"

enjoyment. For one thing, the weather was rainy, foggy and cool. Puddles had collected on the bottom of the skiff, and the burlap cover sagged with moisture. The bargemen seemed ill-humored, swearing and complaining loudly, until General Arnold appeared, when they lapsed into sulky silence. The General himself was in an imperious mood, not content to sit under the canopy, but stalking up and down the deck, giving orders in arrogant, clipped tones.

The big boat pushed off into a current churned by the wind and, despite its size, bobbed and bounced about so violently that Kirby was jostled and giddy. After an hour, his stomach ached. Also he felt as if a fit of sneezing threatened him. Recalling that fateful sneeze of last night, he pressed his finger hard against his upper lip.

He was not sleepy this early in the morning, nor could he relax. Time dragged interminably. Kirby could not estimate its progress because in the segment of gray sky visible to him no sun shone. When he dared to raise himself and glance out, over the side, the river banks were obscured by mist.

The barge had been in motion for perhaps three hours, and rain was pouring, when Kirby heard the General shout: "What dock is that on our right, Ben?"—and a man, answering: "Haverstraw, sir."

Haverstraw! Then they had passed Mr. Smith's house! And where were they bound?

Consternation surged in Kirby's heart and, forgetting caution, he sat straight up, his head bumping the burlap. He must get out of here! He must get out immediately! It did not matter if General Arnold knew that he was a stowaway. Nothing mattered, except that with every sweep of the oars he was being carried farther from home.

He was fumbling with the fastenings of the sodden cloth

—and just then, quite near, a shot reverberated, and another shot, the reverberation of a cannon.

In an instant panic overwhelmed the barge and every person on it.

"We're fired on, sir!" cried the men. "It's gunboats attacking!" "They're the small craft from the *Vulture*, sir!" "Look, you can see—"

"Stick to your oars!" roared General Arnold. "Pull! Draw in to the west bank!"

A shower of lead peppered and hissed in the water, and there was the sound of wood splintering.

"Run up your colors, sir!" begged a voice.

"I have no colors." General Arnold was under the canopy now, shielding himself with the chairs and benches, still roaring. "And if I had, they'd never be seen through this rain. Yes, it's the *Vulture's* gunboats. Pull, men! Make for the shore!"

The barge, abruptly swerving, was like a great unwieldy animal wallowing in midstream. Lead showered again; one support of the canopy snapped and collapsed. The barge dipped.

That was when Kirby slid out of the skiff, stood up, lost his balance, rolled, and went with a splash into the river.

The water closed over him, he sank down and down. Then he was up, sputtering, gasping for air, glancing wildly about him. The barge by this time had swung away; he could not reach it. Instinctively and blindly he struck out toward a bluff and trees dimly outlined against the curtains of fog. He swam with all his might, straining every muscle—and he was a good swimmer! Sooner than he would have thought possible, his feet touched firm rock; the water was neck-deep, then waist-deep, and then he had waded out entirely, to drop exhausted upon the ground.

After a minute he cupped his hands around his eyes and

tried to see the barge. There had been no more firing and the rain had slackened. He could make out the indistinct contours of several boats pushing southward. Those were the gunboats from the British sloop, the *Vulture*, ordinarily at anchor off Kingsbridge many miles to the south. They were going back now. And why had they been sent patrolling up the river this morning?

Kirby peered once more. There was the barge! What was that which was being lowered over the side? The skiff! A man was leaping into it, and another; and the skiff was moving in to the shore.

"It's General Arnold!" murmured Kirby. "He's left the barge; it's too slow; he's looking for cover. Lucky that I got out when I did! Wouldn't the General have been surprised if I hadn't? *Whew!*"

Kirby's eyes followed the skiff as it coursed through the water and came to rest at a point of land downstream. He saw the two figures climbing out now, climbing the bluff, on high ground and vanishing among the trees.

Then Kirby began to think about himself. Where was he? On the west bank of the Hudson, that he knew; and below Haverstraw. The forest behind him looked rather familiar. He rose. He was pretty certain he could find his way home.

But it would be a long, wet walk!

13

A LADY AND SOME LETTERS

ON SEPTEMBER FIFTEENTH, ROBINSON'S HOUSE WAS IN A PERfect hubbub, for this was the day when Mistress Arnold was scheduled to arrive.

She had been a fortnight on the way, with Major David Franks, a sergeant and a squad of infantrymen to escort her and a personal maid to wait upon her. Yet even with all this attention her husband had thought it necessary to write detailed instructions as to the various stages of the journey, how far she must travel each day; and where she should sleep each night, with people of position who could give her luxurious lodging. She must have two carriages to ride in, an open one for fine weather, a closed one for those intervals when chill breezes might blow. Both carriages were to be provisioned with bottles of pure drinking water and hampers of nourishing but dainty food; both must be padded with swansdown pillows so that she would not be jarred by the bumpy roads.

Then, when he knew that she had started, General Arnold had sent out a dragoon to act as special guard in sections where the cowboys and skinners were most troublesome; and he himself had gone to Mr. Joshua Smith's house, to greet her there.

Now the entire party was coming up the river, General and Mistress Arnold on the barge, which had lately been repaired and decorated for the occasion; and all the others crowded into a fleet of smaller boats, like a miniature flotilla, to flank the barge.

Extra soldiers had been summoned from West Point to help Catherine Martin and Emmeline, and the house and lawn were put in order. By noon everything was ready, Catherine and Emmeline in starchy aprons and caps, Colonel Varick in a fresh uniform, his hair combed sleekly back, his boots burnished. Emmeline had wanted to go down to Beverley Dock to see the landing; but Catherine said that was not seemly.

"We'll wait here on the veranda. Mind, you curtsy and don't speak a word unless she speaks to you. It's a lovely day—that's a mercy!" said Catherine.

Emmeline sat on the step—primly, so that she would not muss her apron—and entertained herself by imagining what Mistress Arnold must be like, to have so much care and tenderness lavished upon her. At half-past two there were sounds of voices and rustlings along the path. Emmeline stood up, expectantly.

Marching into the yard were General Arnold, Major Franks, and four of the infantrymen who bore on their shoulders a litter, mounted on poles. In the litter, reclining on cushions, rode a lady with a baby in her arms. Behind her, also marching, were a maidservant and an elderly, portly man. The man was Mr. Hugg.

So amazed was Emmeline to see Mr. Hugg again that she nearly missed the sight of Mistress Arnold being assisted from her cushions by the General, the Major—and Colonel Varick, who hastened forward, bowing gallantly. What was the odd Mr. Hugg doing here? But then Emmeline looked from him to the lady.

"How young she is," thought Emmeline, "and frail— it's no wonder she couldn't walk that marshy path! She's quite pretty, with her pink-and-white complexion, and her eyes so large and her costume so fashionable. Her hair is powdered and beautifully dressed. How does she ever get it up so high, piled on her head, with all the ornaments and jeweled pins, and topped with the feathered bonnet? The coiffure makes her seem lots taller than she really is. I suppose the baby is too bundled in blankets to be seen."

"Curtsy," muttered Catherine, with a nudge of her elbow.

Emmeline curtsied.

Mistress Arnold had given over the baby to the maid. Her gloved hand on the General's wrist, she glided gracefully across the veranda, bestowing a cordial word or two upon Catherine, and nodding an acknowledgment of Emmeline's curtsy.

"They'll want their food," said Catherine, as the Arnolds and the two officers went into the house. "The menfolk in the dining room. Mistress Arnold will probably go right to bed, to rest; and she'll have her tray upstairs. Unless my memory fails me, there'll be much running and fetching to be done. First off, Emmeline, get that letter which came by courier this morning from General Washington, and present it to the master."

When Emmeline had taken the letter, sealed imposingly with wax, to General Arnold, she went to the kitchen where Mr. Hugg was sitting, stout and dignified (and, as Emmeline thought, exactly like an old turtle!) while Catherine stirred up the fire and clattered kettles.

"That maid of Mistress Arnold's is already screeching for things," grumbled Catherine. "Hot water, hot milk, barley broth, tea! Our work is just beginning, Emmeline."

In the evening Colonel Varick, at his desk in the small chamber adjoining the library, glanced up to see Major Franks at the door.

"Ah, hello, Franks."

"I mustn't interfere, Colonel—"

"No, come in. My writing is done, for the nonce."

"The lists?"

"The *interminable* lists. Tell me about Philadelphia. Have you tobacco for your pipe?"

Major Franks sat down. The room was dusky with twilight, and all the house wrapped in peace.

Colonel Varick stuffed the bowl of his own pipe. "Shall we have a candle?"

"No, let's not." Franks smoked in silence a moment. Then he said: "Philadelphia is tense with the feeling that we must win this war—and that we may not. The times are crucial."

"Was there any gaiety in the city?"

"I didn't look for gaiety." He paused. "Varick, I'm dissatisfied. When the destiny of my country is at stake, it's not enough for me to be squiring a charming and impetuous woman hither and yon. I've been with Arnold for three years. Perhaps that's too long."

"You're ambitious, Major."

"It may be." Franks shrugged. "The General's temper doesn't improve; he is constantly more irritable and faultfinding. I used to think I understood him, but now he bewilders me. I'd like to be transferred to the field."

"For selfish reasons, I hope you won't be," Varick said. "You sustain me here."

Franks leaned forward. "Then you're aware of it, too? This feeling of—of catastrophe impending?"

"Oh, I should scarcely call it that, Franks."

"But what is it? Just *what?*"

Varick got up, shut the door, and went back to his chair. "There are little things that indicate some bigger—confusion, shall we say? Straws in the wind. By themselves they're insignificant. But—" He hesitated. "For instance, that part of the correspondence which I am never allowed to read. The General communicates regularly with Mr. Joshua Hett Smith, and with a man named John Anderson in New York City. And now he writes to Colonel Robinson, too. Robinson, whose house this is, claims openly to be a Loyalist and has been made a British officer; Smith is thought to be a Loyalist. As for Anderson, he has never been identified. General Arnold says such a correspondence is advantageous to him and that by it, he'll bring off some triumph. That may be so."

"Or may not be so. And, just the same, there's peril in it."

"Because of Arnold's past record?"

"Yes. He can ill afford an acquaintance with such people, Varick. Tell me," Franks said earnestly, "did you ever doubt that he was guiltless of the crimes they charged him with at the court-martial?"

"Never! My faith in him has been complete. Have you doubted, Major?"

"No. I've *believed* in him. Implicitly."

Colonel Varick drew upon his pipe. "I wonder if he has proposed a meeting with this Anderson."

"He would surely not do that! A man in his position meeting secretly with some unknown person who calls himself John Anderson?"

"It has seemed to me that he intended to transact business with Anderson the day he went down the river and was fired upon by the *Vulture* gunboats."

"That was a dramatic happening, wasn't it?"

"Dramatic, and it might have been tragic. Arnold had no colors on the barge and, of course, no arms except the pistols of the bargemen and his own sword. Fortunately, he got away to the blockhouse on the west bank and returned home from there. But," Varick said hesitantly,

"I've been told that Colonel Beverley Robinson and a stranger were seen that day near Dobbs Ferry. I've wondered if the stranger was John Anderson—and if a meeting had been planned; the General, the Loyalist colonel and this Anderson, whoever he may be."

"Why should the *Vulture* have fired upon him?"

"Why not, Franks? He was below the American outposts and he had no white banner."

"He might have been killed!"

"The marvel is that he wasn't. But you know Benedict Arnold, Franks. He isn't one to fear death—or to have his plans scotched. If he wants to meet Anderson, he'll try until he does meet him."

"The transaction must be important," commented Franks.

"If, indeed, there is a transaction—as, against my will, I am forced to believe."

"We have so many 'ifs' to contend with," said the Major.

For a while they said nothing more. The room darkened and the brassy autumn foliage of a beech bough tapped gently on the windowpane.

Varick put down his pipe. "There is something else."

"Yes?"

"When I came to Robinson's House, it was not to be a caterer or a steward, or to superintend the rationing of either the troops or the General's family. The keys were given to Catherine Martin—by my request. I supposed that she would keep them. Now I find that there is one key which Catherine never has had, one large storeroom in the basement under us which she never enters. General Arnold and a soldier or two from the fort go into that room—and no one else. They go at night. They bring to the room immense amounts of dried food, flour, sugar and wine."

"How do you know this?" The Major's voice was brusque with amazement.

"I've seen it, and I've inquired of Catherine Martin. And I have thought about it."

"A storeroom filled with food and wine?"

"No, not filled. Never filled. The provisions are taken out again, and I don't know how they're disposed of or where they go. They come from the West Point garrison; they have been purchased by the Congress for the troops. They do not belong to any individual; they cannot rightfully be sold or traded by any individual. Selling or trading the army's provisions would be a criminal offense, Franks."

"If it could be proved. But could you—"

"No, I could not prove it. I hope I'll never be asked to. And yet—you remember Philadelphia, Franks?"

"I do. It was selling civilian property then, and pocketing the profits. But there was no conviction. That charge was dropped."

Another silence—and at that instant they saw a man sauntering beneath the window, his thick figure blacker than the shadows.

"Mr. Hugg," said Major Franks. "He managed the transportation of Mistress Arnold's trunks, and he's to carry back some messages of our arrival to her Pennsylvania relatives. An honest fellow, Hugg—or so General Arnold vows. But it was after he was at Robinson's House that the chain in the Hudson was damaged."

Colonel Varick rose and lighted a candle. "I'll wager that the messages Hugg carries are those I shall not see." In the saffron glow he looked steadily at Major Franks, and the Major looked as steadily at him.

Meantime, in the library, General Arnold drove his quill pen furiously, writing, writing. Long ago he had lighted candles, seven of them in a branched holder; their points of flame were mirrored in his flashing eyes. His cheeks were flushed, and the collar of his silken robe was no blacker than his hair. From above came the murmur of a woman's voice, a baby's shrill cry. Peggy and his tiny son! He smiled to hear the sounds.

Four letters he had written.

The first was to General Washington, protesting against His Excellency's order that the eight men who acted as Arnold's bargemen be released from that employment to join their regiment. General Arnold had work for the eight; he hoped the commander-in-chief would agree to their being detained at Robinson's House until the work should be finished.

The second letter was for Major Tallmadge at North Castle . . . "If Mr. John Anderson, a person I expect from New York, should come to your quarters, I have to request that you will give him an escort of two horsemen, to bring him on his way to this place . . ."

The third letter, very lengthy, was phrased in what General Arnold had once referred to as a "mercantile style of writing." The person to whom it was addressed was never named in the text, but he was urged "to come," and assured that he would be in no danger.

"It will be necessary for you to be disguised and if the enemy's boats are there it will favor my plan . . . My partner has £10,000 cash in hand ready for a speculation if any should offer which appears profitable. I have about £1,000 and can collect £1,500 more in two or three days. Add to this I have some *credit*—from these hints you can judge of the purchase that can be made."

Before penning the last of his letters, General Arnold

had read again General Washington's note of that day, especially noting the postscript:

"I shall be at Peekskill on Sunday evening on my way to Hartford," wrote Washington. "You will be pleased to send down a guard of a captain and 50 at that time, and direct the quartermaster to have a night's forage for about 40 horses. You will keep this to yourself, as I want to make my journey a secret."

Painstakingly General Arnold set himself to copying this postscript. But it was a conglomeration of figures and not words which flowed from his pen, six lines of figures, spaced by dots: "*120.9.14..286.9.33.*"

He folded the sheets, sorted them. Two would go by ordinary courier; the other two would be entrusted to honest Mr. Hugg.

Leaning back in his chair, General Arnold thought about the war. There had been more than three years of it; there might be three years more. A wearisome ordeal—and needless! One brave man of genius with one clever stroke could end it in a day, and thus spare the sufferings of innumerable thousands. One single quick, decisive, climactic stroke! Risky, perhaps? But with what rich and glorious results!

And the time was *now*.

14

ARGUMENTS AND STRIFE

AS CATHERINE MARTIN ONCE HAD PROPHESIED, ROBINSON'S House altered with the coming of Mistress Arnold. Not only were the tasks doubled (for it was a fact that the lady required a deal of waiting on—and the new maid, whose name was Bolton, almost as much!) but the very atmosphere of the mansion seemed different. That first night the rooms blazed with candles, vases of russet leaves and goldenrod and purple ironweed adorned the mantels, the gentlemen wore their finest uniforms; and when Mistress Arnold's trailing satin skirts swept down the stairs, she led the way to a table laid artfully by Catherine with silver, china, and crystal goblets.

"There!" Catherine had said. "It's the best *I* can do to help her like the wilderness."

But Catherine had expended effort on the food, too. It was delicious—so good, indeed, that even the smell of it made Emmeline quite weak with hunger, as she trotted in and out with bowls and platters. The wine was the choice of General Arnold's stock. Emmeline thought that Catherine would surely have been disappointed to see how little of the feast seemed to appeal to Mistress Arnold, who only tasted the pheasant and chestnuts, the compote and the tart, and sipped fastidiously at the sherry, her slender fingers curled around the fragile stem of the glass, her eyes meltingly beautiful above the brim.

While the gentlemen ate and drank, Mistress Arnold

smiled at them. Her manner with Colonel Varick was mildly coquettish—later that young man got out his violin and, in his chamber, played a whole program of melancholy tunes.

General Arnold seemed determined that his lovely Peggy should not find this place too dull. He said he had invited Mr. and Mistress Joshua Smith and their nephew to spend a few days at Robinson's House. The Smiths had shown the Arnolds such hospitality as must be repaid in kind; and Mistress Smith, herself a lady of fashion, could console Peggy in this rough, though picturesque, exile.

"And," said the General, "I've asked some of the West Point officers for an early dinner on Sunday. We shall be gay, Peggy."

Afterward, thinking of that week-end, Emmeline questioned the General's use of the adjective. The gathering on Sunday was anything but gay. In fact, the Smiths had no sooner set foot upon the premises than a plague of small mishaps descended. The baby had a spell of colic and screamed so loudly as to cause Mistress Arnold to suffer a splitting headache; the maid, Bolton, quarreled with Catherine; a soldier from the fort, sent to pick apples for baking, tumbled out of the tree and broke his ankle; the farmer from the neighborhood failed to deliver the butter and eggs.

By Sunday, when the officers came from West Point, altercations had arisen between members of the household and the guests. Colonel Varick, usually so polite, was almost openly hostile to Mr. Smith. Major Franks was moody. General Arnold, displeased with both his aides, attempted to smooth over their sulkiness and be the courteous host. Mr. Smith was noisy and made silly jokes at which nobody laughed.

Matters were not mended by the arrival of a letter for

General Arnold at noon on Sunday. The letter was from Beverley Robinson and was delivered as they all sat at the dinner table. General Arnold read it and put it into his pocket. Then, seeing the eyes of everyone upon him, he said casually: "Colonel Robinson desires an interview with me."

Colonel Varick scowled; Major Franks frowned; and one of the West Point officers remarked: "Seems to me that if the Tory has anything to say, he might write it, rather than expose you, sir, to a face-to-face encounter."

"Colonel Robinson wishes to consult with me about repairs on his residence."

"Ah?" said the officer, "then he *could* write it."

The General's smile was rather small and he quickly spoke of something else.

When the awkward meal had ended, Arnold beckoned Colonel Varick to his desk. "I've a task for you," he said. "As you know, Major Franks and I leave within the hour to meet General Washington at Peekskill. I wish you to see to affairs here."

"Very well, sir."

"There must be no lack of civility to the Smiths, Varick."

The Colonel said nothing.

"I shall answer Robinson's missive at once. Please take my dictation."

Colonel Varick got his pen and paper. The General dictated for a moment—and Varick laid down his pen.

"If I may say so, sir, this answer seems more like that of a friend than of an enemy." Varick's face was red to the roots of his sandy hair. "I—I do not approve of it, sir."

General Arnold had been pacing the hearth-rug. "Eh?" He swung around. "What—"

"Beverley Robinson is a Tory, as you were reminded at

dinner. An enemy of our country, therefore your enemy and mine."

General Arnold looked at his secretary. "I said, didn't I, that Robinson's Loyalist tendencies are not in point? This house is his; he wants to discuss it with me."

"In that case, it would be wiser to discuss it publicly with him—or to have his ideas in writing, so any interested person could read them. I do not like his proposal of a private interview."

Arnold resumed his pacing. He shook his head. "I vow, Varick, you're a queer chap. And you are presumptuous, too!"

"I'm thinking of you, sir."

"Oh, are you? Is that why you interfere so often?"

"Yes, sir," said Varick.

After a silence, the General smiled, rather sardonically. "Perhaps you're right . . . Well, then, you write a letter which suits you. I'll sign it. Give it to me to seal."

The General flung himself down at a table and he wrote also, as Varick was writing. When the letter was handed to him for his signature, Arnold folded it slowly and with great care.

"Give me that stick of sealing-wax from the bottom drawer, Colonel Varick." As his secretary stooped to peer into the bottom drawer, Arnold walked over to the window, holding the letter in his hand.

"There isn't any wax here." Varick was rummaging fruitlessly.

"No? Oh, I remember now. In the top drawer, isn't it?" He heated the stick in the candle flame and sealed the papers tight. "Well, you were none too cordial, Colonel, with Beverley Robinson. A very stilted rejoinder."

"You said it was to suit me. It does, sir."

The General laughed a little. "Send it off by a courier. And lose no time."

When the General had gone, Varick sat at the desk, turning the sealed letter in his fingers. It made a packet somewhat thicker than might have been expected; it was quite bulky, yet it contained a single sheet. Varick looked across to the table where General Arnold had sat writing; he saw no paper there. Perhaps the General had slipped his own piece of writing—whatever it was—into his coat. Or—

"My head was bent for a minute," Varick thought. "My attention was engaged with the bottom drawer. And he was at the window. I suppose he *could* have—"

Varick rubbed at his forehead and blinked. "No, no! He *couldn't* have. I'm imagining things. An absurd notion!"

He called a soldier who would act as courier, and he sent the letter off.

"Poor Mr. Richard!" said Catherine Martin to Emmeline. "I'm sorry for him. He has no hankering for the society of that Mr. Smith—and he must pretend to be genial."

It was tea-time; General Arnold and Major Franks had ridden away and the officers had returned to West Point. Colonel Varick, Mistress Arnold and the Smiths were in the drawing-room, cups balanced on their knees—and had Catherine overheard the conversation there, she would have realized that poor Mr. Richard was just on the brink of abandoning geniality.

The sight of Mr. Joshua Smith, ruddy and fat and sleek in his broadcloth coat and silk stockings, filled Colonel Varick with loathing, for Mr. Smith seemed to typify everything a soldier most feared and detested. General Arnold had said that his secretary must be civil; Colonel Varick had tried to be, but Mr. Smith's words were not soothing; they were no better than his looks.

"This fellow is like one of those round, pasty-white worms in a walnut!" thought Colonel Varick. "And he has no more intelligence, either!"

"There is really no excuse, Mistress Arnold," Mr. Smith was saying, "for the prolonging of the war. The colonists might have made an honorable peace with Great Britain when the commissioners came from England in 1778."

Mistress Arnold did not reply, but Colonel Varick said distinctly: "That is not so."

"The country is sick and tired of war. No one wants war."

"I do," said Colonel Varick. "I want it, if by war we can gain our independence."

"Americans, my dear sir, are a people devoted to peace."

"They are. And resolved to win it—a peace with freedom. Nothing less will satisfy them."

Mr. Smith fastidiously stirred his tea, the spoon clicking in the cup. "As for myself, I am a man of peace."

"And *my* opinion is that in these times the only men of peace are cowards."

Mistress Arnold swiftly raised her head. "Colonel Varick!"

"Your pardon, madam."

"Ah, my dear lady," said Mr. Smith, with a smile, "the young man is not so ferocious as he sounds."

"I am *quite* ferocious." Colonel Varick was trembling. "I repeat my statement. The only men who put peace above freedom and independence are cowards and I condemn them."

"You are a very warm and stanch patriot, sir."

"I am. And I have no tolerance for any person who is not."

"Colonel Varick!" exclaimed Mistress Arnold, again.

"If I had my way, I would put in custody every able-bodied man in America who is not now bearing arms or contributing some other service to our sacred cause."

Mr. Smith smiled imperturbably. "You are not bearing arms at the moment. You are fortunately far from the fighting."

"I am most *unfortunately* far from the front line of defense, yes. But I am serving my country, sir, and I challenge you to deny it."

"Challenge? Well, well," said Mr. Smith, "a harsh term."

"*Do* you challenge it?"

Mistress Arnold got suddenly to her feet. She pressed her hand to her bosom. "I must retire," she said. "I am weary."

"And I, too," said Mistress Smith who, all this while, had been sitting, decorous and lady-like, beside her husband.

The gentlemen jumped up and Colonel Varick took the tea cups and ranged them carefully on the tray. The bow with which he bade the others good night was very stiff—and he glared at Mr. Smith who still smiled and seemed entirely calm.

Colonel Varick was alone in the room when Emmeline came to remove the tea things. He was sprawled in a chair, his long legs extended, his chin sunk into his shirt ruffles; and he was so motionless that Emmeline did not at first see him. But then he sighed.

"I beg your pardon, sir!" Emmeline was startled.

He turned his head. "Oh, it's you, Emmeline."

"Yes, sir. Am I disturbing you?"

"Not at all."

She straightened the furniture and picked up a napkin from the floor. "Colonel Varick?"

"Yes?"

"There is something I have been meaning to ask you. About a letter."

"A letter? Whose?"

"That's what I don't know, sir. It is one which was in the cellar. I asked Catherine Martin about it, and Major Franks too. It doesn't belong to them—or, of course, to me. I want to give it back. Having it has troubled me."

She had been carrying the letter in the belt of her sprigged muslin frock. She got it out, the crumpled bit of paper, and offered it to him.

"I—I read it. I should not have done that, and I apologize. But I didn't understand it, sir."

He was bending over, looking at the paper by the light of the fire in the grate. "No," he said, "you would not have understood it. It is in cipher."

"Is it yours, Colonel Varick?"

"No, not mine."

She hesitated. "That name, sir. There is no one here named *Gustavus*."

"No one, Emmeline," he said, and threw the letter into the fire.

As the flames licked up to consume it, a rumbling was heard, a dull reverberation, loud and louder, and then subsiding.

"What was that?" demanded Colonel Varick.

"Thunder, sir."

"But the night is clear."

"Oh, we often have it so, here in the Highlands. Some people," said Emmeline, "the superstitious folk, think it's an omen. But most of us know it's just—thunder."

15

JED RIDES TO PEEKSKILL

JED CONSIDERED HIMSELF LUCKY TO BE RIDING TO PEEKSKILL with Washington and Lafayette, even though his own place in the company was a very humble one. He had been detailed to look after the French general's horse, a blooded and skittish animal, which required expert management. Once before, while troops were ferrying, the horse had become terrified at the sight of water and, breaking away, had plunged headlong into the river. This was General Lafayette's favorite mount; the incident must not recur today, when King's Ferry should be reached.

"I want a man with a strong hand and a gentle manner," Lafayette had said to the sergeant; and the sergeant had replied: "Aye, sir, that'll be young Drake, as steady a lad as ever I've seen."

The weather was fine and riding was a pleasure. Jed liked the look of the tilted fields, just browning with autumn's beginning; he liked the rainbow hues of the trees which frost had touched. The sky was blue and mottled with frothy clouds; the quiet hills were green below and tufted above with shades of copper and bronze. All the landscape was familiar to Jed, and so beloved; the little stone houses, the barns and fences gave him the feeling of home. Across the river (not far!) was Donderberg and Granny's cottage.

"But for the bluffs I might see our poor old crooked chimney!" he said to himself.

As they approached Peekskill, General Washington was in the lead, his flowing black cloak billowing back from his sturdy shoulders. His three-cornered hat had the sheen of velvet where the sun struck it, and the metal of his harness, his sword hilt and spurs glittered dazzlingly. Just behind him rode Colonel Alexander Hamilton, slender and elegant, and General Lafayette, small, dapper, his figure aristocratic, his youthful face tinged with health and vigor.

"I would follow such men anywhere," thought Jed devoutly. "I would follow them to death."

As the cavalcade neared the town, more soldiers rode out to meet them, the escort from West Point with General Arnold himself and a major in front. When the escort drew up in respectful formation, General Arnold and his aide came on, saluting, to receive His Excellency's recognition.

It was Jed's first view of General Arnold. He scanned him carefully, this dark handsome man, with bold features and eyes almost unnaturally brilliant. The officer with him was stalwart and tanned, but not tall, and his countenance was undistinguished except for the scar on his chin.

"It's Major Franks," guessed Jed; and from what Emmeline had told him, he knew that the Major must be a courteous gentleman.

After an interval of greetings, the Generals, Colonel Hamilton and Major Franks rode toward the river. At a signal from Lafayette, Jed fell in with the little procession—though keeping several paces behind it. They went up the bluff to the plateau overlooking the Hudson and there they halted. Jed jumped down, tethered his own horse and hastened to stand beside General Lafayette in an attitude of attention.

"It is well, Drake," said General Lafayette, slipping from the saddle, "to be watchful, eh? The steady lad with the firm hand on the bridle of this beautiful, crazy steed of mine!"

General Washington dismounted, and then General Arnold. Jed noticed that Arnold, as he walked, limped slightly. That was from Saratoga, of course. An honorable wound, the relic of heroism, of pain and sacrifice endured for the sake of an ideal and a country. If Jed's head had not already been bared, he would have swept off his battered hat in awe and reverence.

General Washington had produced his spy-glass. He raised it and surveyed the river. The air was clear and clean, his gaze unobstructed.

"That ship," he said. "The *Vulture?*"

"Yes, Your Excellency," replied Arnold.

"So it has moved up from Spuyten Duyvil?"

"To Teller's Point, yes."

"A rash advance, it seems to me, in waters in which a British sloop should not dare to venture. How do you explain it, Arnold?"

"I cannot. I am quite at a loss to conjecture, sir. The *Vulture* moved in the night, or so I am told."

Washington looked again through the glass. "I do not like to think that the sloop can go up or down the Hudson, at will. Her commander must have a reason for such audacity."

"There could be no reason but the audacity itself, Your Excellency."

As Washington was silent, half turned away, his head lifted, Arnold seemed to glance nervously at the chief's profile, magnificently proud, magnificently stern. Then, in a cautious voice, Arnold said:

"I implore your counsel, sir, in a matter, trifling perhaps, but which has puzzled me. I have had a message from Colonel Beverley Robinson. He has asked for an audience with me, to talk over the condition of his house which I am occupying."

General Washington lowered the spy-glass. "His house?"

"The furnishings, proposed improvements—something. My query is, Your Excellency, what must I say to him?"

"To Beverley Robinson, the traitor? Nothing, Arnold. What would you say?"

"Certainly I can think of nothing. But his letter—"

"Do not trouble to respond to it. My counsel is that you have no further dealings with Beverley Robinson."

A slow flush stained Arnold's face; with a gesture he pushed back the black hair from his brow.

"Very good, Your Excellency," he said.

While the Generals were apart, at the edge of the bluff, Jed had been trying to bolster himself to address Major Franks.

He said, at last and shyly: "Sir?"

Major Franks, sitting his horse easily, looked around. "You are speaking to me?"

Jed saluted. "Private Jeremiah Drake, sir. I wanted to inquire about my sister, Emmeline."

"Oh, is Emmeline your sister?"

"Yes, sir. She is at Robinson's House."

"She is, indeed. And very helpful, very industrious, too. We could scarcely do without Emmeline."

"I hope she is well."

"Quite well, I think."

"Would you be good enough to tell her something for me, sir?" As Major Franks nodded, Jed continued: "Say to her, please, that I haven't been able to keep my promises in the pact we made, but that I think I may, even yet. And say that I hope Patience's children have been sold."

"A pact—and the selling of children? It seems rather a

strange item of news. But since you wish it, I will tell your sister."

"Thank you, sir. And," Jed said, "they aren't really children, you know. They're pigs."

"Ah?" exclaimed Major Franks, smiling. "Pigs! I am much relieved."

"Yes, sir. The pigs belong to Kirby; he wants to sell them."

"And who is Kirby?"

"My younger brother." Then, somehow, perhaps because of the Major's friendly smile, Jed was pouring out the whole story of the pact, and the place of the pigs in it, and of his own promises, and Emmy's, and of Granny's situation in the cottage that was so dilapidated. He finished with a question: "Do you think, sir, that my grandmother will be safe from harm in Rhode Island?"

Major Franks had listened soberly. "I think she would be safer there than here, Drake. But war is like a forest fire. It spreads and flares up suddenly in the most unlikely spots. No one can predict its ravages. One of the saddest things about it is that it separates families—and in more ways than one!" He paused. "I am a Canadian, by birth. When I left home to join the army, I knew I was seeing my father for the last time. My father is a British subject and is resolved to remain one, true to the king. He considers me a rebel—and an outcast."

"I am sorry, sir," said Jed softly.

Major Franks shook his head. "But I had to act as my conscience prompted."

"Yes, that was right, sir; the only thing you could do."

They seemed for a moment very close and intimate, these two, the officer and the lean, muscular boy in his shabby regimentals. In this first conversation they seemed like comrades.

"How is the war going, sir?"

"We will win it—eventually, Drake. We'll combine our forces with the French and take New York City. But that means the Hudson forts must be held. If Sir Henry Clinton, the British general, should proceed up the river to West Point or farther, he could cut us off and prevent our uniting with the French. What I say is no military secret, nor have I any confidential information to draw upon. It's just what all observers think, common knowledge."

"Then I am glad," said Jed, "that General Arnold is in charge of the Hudson garrisons. He is a great soldier."

"I have believed that," Major Franks said, deliberately, "for years."

"He doesn't have the word 'defeat' in his vocabulary—or 'surrender,' either."

"No," said Major Franks, and then again, emphatically, as if to clinch an argument—though surely Jed was not arguing: "*No!* . . . He is a great soldier!"

The three Generals, with their accompanying troops, rode down the river path to the eastern terminus of King's Ferry, and there Arnold turned back. He had been agitated and distrait, his nervousness increasing. He had pulled up his horse repeatedly, stopping to glance around him on all sides, his dark eyes fiercely peering into the trees that lined the path, as if he thought some attacker might spring out, or the progress of His Excellency be waylaid. His hand was on the gun thrust into his belt; he frowned and was absent-minded, his wits wool-gathering. Once, at a crash in the forest, he swerved, whipped out the gun, leveled it.

But the sound was only that of a giant oak falling under a woodsman's ax—and George Washington's journey was placid and uninterrupted.

At the ferry Washington said to General Arnold: "I

shall be coming this route again next Sunday, sir, and will lodge with you overnight."

"At Robinson's House? I am honored," said Arnold, bowing, "and my wife will be delighted to be Your Excellency's hostess."

16

AN EVENTFUL DAY—AND NIGHT

IT WAS THURSDAY, SEPTEMBER 21, AND ONCE MORE KIRBY HAD taken the road, bent on visiting the Cahoons and completing a business arrangement which had to do with swine.

Only after some maneuvering had Kirby persuaded Grandmother to let him go, for he had returned in rather bad shape from his former jaunt to Mr. Joshua Smith's estate. Granny had said that this time he must behave more like a respectable person of sense and breeding and less like one of those hoodlum cowboys or skinners.

"No stowing away on anybody's boat, Kirby!"

"Oh, no, Granny."

"And if you must stay all night, see that the Cahoon brothers give you proper shelter."

He arrived at the house of Mr. Samuel Cahoon just before noon. Today both the brothers were at home, sitting outdoors in the grass. Kirby sat down beside them.

The Cahoons were big, burly, black-browed men who had little to say—and said that little mostly with throaty growls and shrugs of the shoulders. Samuel admitted that he wanted to acquire Patience's brood; Joseph commented that Kirby's price was exorbitant. And after these expressions they said nothing at all, but merely sat.

Presently they seemed to forget Kirby and began to converse between themselves.

Samuel Cahoon had a grievance, he was disgruntled.

Last evening, Mr. Joshua Smith had requested Samuel to row him down the river. "To the British sloop," Samuel growled. "She dropped down nigh on to Dobb's Ferry yesterday. All that way I was to row him. I said no."

But Mr. Smith had persevered ("a-dinging and a-danging," Samuel called it) and he had displayed a piece of writing which said that permission was given to Joshua Smith, Esquire, to a gentleman, Mr. John Anderson, and the gentleman's two servants, to pass the guards near King's Ferry at all times.

"Who is this Mr. John Anderson?" Joseph asked.

"Blamed if I know, Joseph."

"Is he aboard the *Vulture?*"

"Seems so. And Mr. Smith has some errand or other with him. The writing," Samuel said, "was from General Arnold up at West Point. It was his hand."

"So you wouldn't row old Smith? No doubt he's too fat to row himself. A whale, and all blubber!" Joseph spat contemptuously. "But later you went off to Robinson's House with Mr. Smith's note to General Arnold. Why was that?"

"It was him a-dinging and a-danging at me. Wouldn't give me any rest! 'Well,' I finally said, 'I'll take your note.' I read it, too; there wasn't much in it, just that Smith couldn't get an oarsman and what was he to do."

"Did General Arnold send back an answer?"

"I never saw the General. I rode hell-for-leather and reached Robinson's House before dawn. I knocked and a tall thin fellow, kind of sandy-like, came and took Smith's note and said there wouldn't be any answer. Don't know who the fellow was, Joseph."

"Oh, it must have been Colonel Varick!" Kirby piped.

The two Cahoons turned their massive heads as one and glowered. And after that, Kirby kept still.

"Now here's General Arnold, a-coming down early this morning in his barge," said Joseph, breaking a lengthy pause. "What do you make of it, Samuel? The General fussing about, him and old Smith running in and out of the house, and nobody else around—"

"They were all hustled off," Samuel said, "even the cook, as soon as Mistress Smith and the nephew went to Boston. That house is empty."

"But what's it mean, Samuel?"

"Something about patriotic service, Mr. Smith told me. You know, don't you, a skiff's been moored in the rushes in Haverstraw Creek, and horses from Smith's stable are tied in the grove, where none'll notice 'em?"

"No! A skiff—and horses? And a patriotic service?"

"Urgent. That was old Smith's word for it. Urgent."

"Humph! This is mighty funny, Samuel."

"*Mighty* funny, Joseph."

Then for a long while the Cahoons uttered no sound.

At two o'clock the brothers got up, walked to the pasture fence and leaned against it.

Kirby walked and leaned, too. "Now, about those pigs."

"I'm studying it over," said Samuel.

"Money's tight," offered Joseph.

At three o'clock they made an inspection tour of the Cahoon orchard.

"My pigs are extra fine."

"I was never a man to be hurried," said Samuel.

"Money'll be scarcer yet," said Joseph. "Scarce as hen's teeth."

At four o'clock Samuel announced that he was going to the lower field to fetch in the cows. And just then Mr. Smith stepped out onto the veranda and waved his arms.

"Samuel," Joseph said, "it's him. The whale. He wants to speak to you, I reckon."

"Oh, lor'!" breathed Samuel. "More of his a-dinging and a-danging."

"Still," Joseph said, "you better see."

As Samuel hesitated, Kirby said: "You go, Mr. Cahoon. Your brother, too. I'll fetch the cows."

Perhaps by being accommodating, Kirby could make a good impression, and a sale.

The Cahoons lumbered toward the house, but only Samuel went in. Joseph squatted on the veranda, pensively twiddling his thumbs.

The upstairs room of the Smith house was shadowy, with the curtains drawn. General Arnold graciously invited Samuel to be seated. Without speaking, Samuel conveyed the idea that he preferred to stand. Mr. Smith was at the door. He looked plump and pompous and excited.

"Cahoon," the General said, omitting preliminaries, "you're taking a little excursion with us tonight."

"Not me, sir. No. I was up the whole of last night. I have to get my sleep."

General Arnold frowned. "You want to serve your country, don't you?"

"If you're asking am I an American—yes, I am. Samuel Cahoon is not one of these pesky Loyalist varmints. Drat 'em!"

"Exactly." General Arnold's frown was less severe. "Then you'll understand me when I say it's your duty to go on our excursion. We must all do our best for our country, mustn't we?"

Samuel shuffled his big feet. "Where is it you aim to go?"

"There's a man on board the *Vulture*, Cahoon. He must be brought ashore to meet me at a certain place."

So it was the same thing, the same fantastic errand?

Samuel was disgusted. "Why can't he stay aboard the *Vulture* till the morning, sir?"

"That is impossible," said the General, and the frown was back between his bright black eyes.

"There's guard boats on the river. They'd not let us by. They might shoot."

The General and Mr. Smith exchanged glances, and Mr. Smith said, with a laugh. "Oh, no! The guard boats are all American. We needn't fear them." He shook his finger. "What I fear is that if you don't consent, you'll be branded as a Loyalist varmint, Samuel."

"That, at least," said General Arnold, "and maybe something worse." He threw back his shoulders and added arrogantly, "Come now, Cahoon. No further dallying. You're going with me and Mr. Smith."

"I've no mind to do it, sir," Samuel said in truculent tones.

"But you must."

"If I could get my brother to say he'd go too—"

General Arnold turned to Mr. Smith. "Bring in his brother. They'll both go."

When Joseph entered, Mr. Smith became the spokesman. This was a legitimate enterprise, he said, very simple, and consisted only of rowing General Arnold to a certain spot on the river bank and then taking Mr. Smith on a bit farther, to the sloop. If ever the Cahoons were criticized, Mr. Smith would clear them.

"You couldn't clear us, sir," Samuel asserted, "if there was aught bad in it."

"Bad?" Mr. Smith laughed heartily. "No, no!"

"Suppose we were stopped by American sentries?" said Joseph.

"I have the countersign. It's *'Congress'*—"

"That will do, Smith!" shouted General Arnold suddenly.

"Oh, I—I'm sorry—" Mr. Smith looked embarrassed.

"We don't pay any attention to your saying 'Congress,' sir. We don't care what the countersign is." Joseph beetled his bushy brows. "I do not choose to go."

"Nor I," said Samuel.

The Cahoons tramped out of the room and down the stairs.

But Mr. Smith would not regard the matter as settled. Not at all. Before fifteen minutes had elapsed he had cornered them again. The brothers were on the stoop of Samuel's house. Tenacious as a gadfly, perspiring, mopping his face with a silk handkerchief, Mr. Smith planted himself in front of them.

The circumstances were not such that the Cahoons could say whether or not they *chose* to go. They had no choice. General Arnold had issued a command; they must obey. The General's friend was on the *Vulture;* it was necessary —absolutely imperative—that he be brought ashore!

"What if I told you that your future and mine—and *everybody's*—hinges on your obeying the General's command tonight?"

The Cahoons were not perturbed about futures.

Three hours later, when the stars were out, Mr. Smith was still at it. The Cahoons were very bored. General Arnold came across the yard, beckoned to Mr. Smith, whispered in his ear.

"Now, men," Mr. Smith said, "you row that boat for the General and he'll give you each fifty pounds of flour."

Flour? It was more precious than gold!

"And if you don't do as you're told, the General will arrest you immediately as traitors. *Traitors!*"

"Well," Samuel muttered unhappily.

AN EVENTFUL DAY—AND NIGHT

And Joseph echoed, "Ah, well." . . .

It was a beautiful night, so tranquil that no ripple stirred the Hudson's breast, the oars muffled in sheepskin dipped rhythmically and made no noise. Six miles downstream, and then across the stretch known as Haverstraw Bay—and there was the *Vulture,* with one lone lamp burning amidship. Mr. Smith clambered up the rope ladder and presented papers to the man who stood at the rail. The papers were the pass which Samuel Cahoon had seen, and a scrap on which was scribbled only a line: *"Gustavus to John Anderson."*

"He's waiting for you, Mr. Anderson," murmured Mr. Smith.

"But I thought," the man said, "he was coming here. That was our agreement."

"I only know he expects you, sir. We had better get underway." Mr. Smith slid awkwardly down into the boat.

The man continued to stand at the rail.

"Hurry, sir!" admonished Mr. Smith.

"It is not as I thought it would be. I was quite sure I should meet him here."

"Please come!" begged Mr. Smith. "All is in readiness."

"Very well," the man said, and without more parley swung down the rope.

Above, another voice said, out of the darkness: "Do you wish one of our boats to tow you part of the way?"

"No, I thank you, Colonel Robinson," Smith answered. "If we were seen with a *Vulture* tow, that might be an infringement of the flag."

The Cahoon brothers pushed off, rowing back across Haverstraw Bay to a landing at the foot of Long Clove Mountain, where, in a rocky indentation of the Hudson's west bank, General Arnold waited.

The man in the stern had been silent; as the Cahoons beached, he leaped out on the shale. Mr. Smith followed; they went up the bluff and were hidden from sight by clustering fir trees. But in a moment Mr. Smith reappeared and got into the boat.

"General Arnold and his friend have a few things to discuss," he said to the Cahoons. "It'll not be more than an hour."

It was more than four hours. Mr. Smith dozed; the Cahoons dozed; the boat rocked idly. When the horizon was streaked with gray, Mr. Smith roused, shivered, gazed at the sky, muttered an exclamation. He got heavily out and went up toward the fir glade. Soon he was back; behind him were General Arnold and his friend.

"Row Mr. Anderson to the *Vulture* without delay," said Arnold.

But the Cahoons were looking at this Mr. Anderson, in the growing light of dawn examining him. He was slender, young, elegantly groomed. He wore a blue caped cloak—and beneath the cloak was the scarlet coat of a British uniform.

"*I'll* never row him!" Samuel said.

"I command you."

"You've commanded enough for once," said Samuel impudently. "I was out all last night on your account. I'll *not* take the gentleman to the sloop, and that I swear!"

"Nor I," said Joseph.

Mr. Smith sighed. "I veritably believe, sir, that these men are quite tired out. I know them. They'll not be cajoled or threatened. Let us all return to my house before the sun rises."

"Then Mr. Anderson will ride with me on the horses yonder," said Arnold. "You come in the boat, Smith."

Mr. Anderson had been gazing from one to another, as

he hugged his enveloping cape about him. "Most unusual!" he said.

"But it is for the best," commented Arnold. "You would not wish to be observed."

"No. And yet—"

"We have not long before the sun will be up."

"Do you prod me, General Arnold? Why, I might almost think that you had foreseen this complication and were not averse to it! That you had even prepared for it—"

"Now, sir, I assure you—"

"Oh, very well. I came in the dark, I shall go in the dark." Mr. Anderson's voice was regretful, but resigned. "Whether one night or the next is now of little consequence, for there is no turning back. Let us ride to Mr. Smith's house."

17

CONFERENCE IN AN UPSTAIRS ROOM

KIRBY WAS WAKENED BY THE LIGHT SHINING IN HIS EYES. The window which he faced looked right into the first level rays of the sun.

But whose window was it?

He sat up—and remembered. This was Mr. Smith's parlor. Kirby had been lying on a damask couch. He was the only living soul in the room, in the house, on the premises.

He knew how he had got here. It all came back to him, his lingering of the night before, how he had waited, clinging to the hope that the Cahoons would finally talk with him—"talk turkey," thought Kirby, though of course it was really pigs! But Samuel and Joseph had been embroiled in that endless wrangle with Mr. Smith and General Arnold; and at last they had all gone off in the Cahoons' boat. For a while then Kirby had wandered about the stable yard, convinced that it was too late to start home yet most uncertain as to where he could spend the remaining hours of darkness. He had seen the open window of Mr. Smith's parlor and, as the chill of the night sharpened, he had reluctantly crawled over the sill. He had not meant to go to sleep. That was purely accidental. But since he had fallen a prey to drowsiness—how fortunate that the couch below the window was soft and that there had been a bearskin rug to pull up over his knees!

He was pleased to recall that he had told Grandmother

CONFERENCE IN AN UPSTAIRS ROOM 149

he might be absent all night and that he had given his word to refrain only from stowing away on anybody's *boat*. This was a house, and surely even Granny (who could be uncompromising at times) must think it a proper shelter.

Kirby's musings were rudely shattered by a detonation somewhere in the distance. When the noise was repeated, again and again, he knew it for cannon fire down the river. Suddenly, with one tremendous explosion, the noise ceased.

Kirby hopped off the couch and replaced the bearskin rug on the floor. It was at that moment he heard another sound—hoofs on the gravel lane. Two horsemen were coming up the drive, General Arnold and a younger, slighter man who was bareheaded and wore a blue cloak.

They were dismounting, tethering the horses and coming into the house. Kirby was quiet. Somehow, he had a dread of encounters with the famous commandant of West Point. Confronted by an interloper in the residence of Mr. Joshua Smith, General Arnold might lose his temper.

"Or," thought Kirby, "I might lose *mine*."

General Arnold had a key which he fitted into the lock. The door swung, and Kirby could hear their voices.

"That fusillade must have been aimed at the *Vulture*," said the General.

"It was a very hot fire."

"Colonel Livingston at Teller's Point has acted impulsively—without orders from me. I trust that your captain and Colonel Beverley Robinson were not hurt. The fact is, Americans have been made suspicious by the sailings of the *Vulture*. Well, Major, we are alone here."

"It would seem so. But Mr. Smith and his servants will soon be with us; and I must beg you to exercise caution in the use of my title."

"Have no fear of that!" General Arnold laughed. "You are John Anderson, the merchant who may apprise me of intelligence valuable to the rebellion. None knows better than I, sir, just how valuable *is* the intelligence!"

"Shall we search these rooms?"

"Oh, there's no need. We'll have privacy."

"And what have you told Mr. Smith?"

"Nothing. Nothing at all beyond the obvious things."

"Is Smith a Loyalist?"

"I wonder," said General Arnold. "I'm not sure. He does not own to it. But he is not a clever man, and so he can be the tool of clever men."

"Does he think I am a spy?"

"A spy? You are not that!"

"No, I am not—but I would be regarded as one. To all appearances, I became a spy the instant I crossed the American lines."

"You should not be in uniform, perhaps." Abruptly General Arnold broke off. "Hark! There's the good Joshua on the garden path. And the Cahoons—stupid louts! Come, my friend, we'll go upstairs where Smith will join us."

Kirby had been squatting behind the parlor door, which was ajar. As the boots of General Arnold and his companion pounded hollowly up the steps, he darted into the hall, thinking to get out of the house before Mr. Smith entered.

But Mr. Smith was already in, and crying: "What's this? Why, it's the Drake boy! And what are you doing here?"

"I wish to see Mr. Samuel Cahoon, sir." Kirby was frightened, for Mr. Smith, who could look either very jolly or very angry, was at his angriest now.

"Cahoon is not in this house. Except for myself—and you—this house is empty!" Mr. Smith paused, and then demanded: *"Isn't* it empty?"

But Kirby, without replying, had sidled to the door, and fled.

CONFERENCE IN AN UPSTAIRS ROOM 151

In the upstairs room where yesterday the Cahoon brothers had debated, General Arnold stood at the window and peered through a spy-glass.

"The *Vulture* is moving downstream."

"There was an attack upon her," declared Mr. Smith, coming in.

"So we thought!"

"Livingston opened fire, and continued until the American powder magazine blew up. The sloop was somewhat damaged, though not badly."

General Arnold nodded. "Probably she'll not resume her former position off Teller's Point. It disrupts my plans, to an extent. In this case, Mr. Anderson must find another route of return, for he has no desire to remain here overlong. I suggest that he cross the river and go southward by land, catching up with the *Vulture* below Dobb's Ferry —or going on, by the roads, to New York City."

Mr. Anderson lifted his head alertly. His countenance was boyish and sensitive in the light which sifted through the lowered blinds. His bearing was erect and soldierly; and, for all his slenderness, there was an air of strength about him.

"A moment ago you said I was to go as I came, in the boat."

"I said that, yes." Arnold nodded again. "But now that the *Vulture* has sailed, such a course would be imprudent."

"I fear the course thus far has been imprudent. Mr. Smith, I appeal to you. Will you not escort me back tonight as I was brought—in the boat?"

Mr. Smith coughed, his eyes sought the General's eyes, and he mutely shook his head.

"You will not? And the General will not?" Mr. Anderson smiled rather oddly. "Then I'm virtually your prisoner here."

"Nothing of the sort!" Arnold exclaimed.

"And can the prisoner escape?"

"My dear sir," Arnold said, "I'll write a pass and Mr. Smith will conduct you to the east shore and through the pickets."

"A pass?"

"Or passes. As many as are required, on whatever roads you like. I'll write them this minute. A pen, Mr. Smith!"

"There are pens and ink on the table, sir."

The General seated himself and wrote. He got up and handed several papers to Mr. Anderson who stood, posed negligently before the mantel. "I have included a permit by which you may go in a boat—if one should be available, Mr. Anderson."

"Thank you." The young man bowed. He merely glanced at the papers. "But your opinion is that no boat *will* be available?"

"To be frank, I fear not, sir. Those documents I delivered to you last night—how will you carry them?"

"I haven't decided. Perhaps you have a suggestion, General?"

"They must be concealed on your person," Arnold said. "Put them between your stockings and your feet."

"Inside my stockings? I'd never have thought of it! But then I haven't your experience in this sort of thing. No one would dream of looking for the documents there, eh?"

"Should any mischance befall you, the documents must be immediately destroyed. Immediately."

"If I were going by boat, I could tie them with string, weight them with a rock—"

Arnold interrupted, frowning. "I suppose so. But if you go by land—"

"Which seems more likely, doesn't it?" The odd smile

twisted Mr. Anderson's lips. "Very well, sir. Between my stockings and my feet. I agree to this and to all your proposals. It would be futile not to. If mischance befalls me, I destroy the cause of it."

"As to a disguise—"

"Now that," Mr. Anderson said, "I'll not agree to! I shall travel in my own clothing."

"Your scarlet coat?"

"And all the rest of it, sir."

"No, no! What folly to court disaster! You would be marked at once."

There was a little silence in which Mr. Anderson seemed to meditate. And Joshua Smith said: "The General is right. If I'm to go with you, I'd rather you had on another coat. After all, sir, you're only a merchant *pretending* to be a British officer. And there's no good in keeping up the pretense—why, there may be harm!"

Mr. Anderson looked closely at Smith. "You're positive I *am* just pretending to be a British officer, aren't you?"

"Oh, certainly. Oh, quite."

"And what, I wonder, are you pretending to be, Mr. Smith?"

"I pretend nothing. I don't have to." Mr. Smith puffed out his cheeks pompously. "I am General Arnold's helper in a patriotic service."

"Let's not waste time," said the General irritably. "Perhaps Mr. Smith has a coat you can borrow."

This silence was longer. Mr. Anderson walked to the window and back; he drummed his fingers on the mantel. "Very well then. I borrow from Mr. Smith. It's all of one piece, isn't it? And all most surprising to me. I never thought last night, as I awaited you on the *Vulture's* deck— but your logic seems unanswerable. Perhaps a man in my situation is not privileged to see into the future."

"What do you mean, Mr. Anderson?" queried Mr. Smith

"Oh, nothing. What should I mean?"

"I assure you," General Arnold said, with a cheery smile "that everything will work out with the utmost ease."

"For you, General? Or for me?"

"For all of us! We have accomplished a *coup* of great brilliance. We have made history in these hours together and we must congratulate ourselves. And you, sir, have no reason in the world to doubt that you'll reach your destination unmolested."

"My destination, by land, on roads I'm not acquainted with? If I *were* molested, what then of the brilliant *coup?*"

"Please put that out of your thoughts!" General Arnold's smile deepened and was indomitable, as if with it he would charm away Mr. Anderson's obscure misgivings. "You may ride the same horse you rode this morning. I remember you said you liked that horse. Well, he's yours. Mr. Smith has been stabling him for me. I make you a present of him."

"The horse is a fine animal, and you are generous, sir." The young man's eyes held a rather mocking expression. "But why do you pick up your hat? You're not leaving us?"

"Yes, I must. I'm sorry." General Arnold set his hat on his head. "I should like so much to remain a while. I have an enormous amount of business to see to at West Point today. My barge is due at the dock. I can't neglect my official obligations, Mr. Anderson, even for the enjoyment of your society."

"Naturally not."

If there was irony in Mr. Anderson's cultivated voice, General Arnold seemed not to notice. He clapped a hand on Mr. Anderson's shoulder. "My prayers and best wishes go with you. *Au revoir,* sir!"

Mr. Anderson looked steadily at him and said, "Goodby, General Arnold."

Joshua Smith ceremoniously saw Arnold to the door,

and then stumped up the stairs again. Mr. Anderson was ambling idly about the room, staring at the pictures on the walls, humming softly to himself.

"It's high time we had a bit of rest." Mr. Smith sat down; he was breathing fast from unwonted exertion, and his face was creased with weariness. "There's your bed, sir, and I can vouch for its being comfortable."

Mr. Anderson raised his eyebrows. "Then we don't start at once?"

"Oh, no. Not until evening—and darkness. Wasn't that what you yourself said?"

"Perhaps I did. Much has been said; I'm probably a bit muddled. But somehow I begin to be impatient here."

"What would be the sense in hurrying when we're both fagged out?"

"No sense at all, I suppose. I am losing track of sense."

Mr. Smith spread blunt, thick hands on his knees. "We'll ferry to Verplanck's Point and chat with Colonel Livingstone there."

"The American commander? Would that be wise—in the circumstances?"

"Why not?"

"Why not, indeed? You amaze me, Mr. Smith. I amaze myself."

"Then we'll jog to Crompound, where'll we sleep?"

"*You* may sleep at Crompound, Mr. Smith. I shall go on to White Plains."

"Oh, well, if you prefer to." Mr. Smith yawned. "I was intending to cross the Hudson anyway, tomorrow. My wife and nephew will be on the stage from Boston. I want to meet them at the ferry. So I shall just kill two birds with one stone."

"My dear sir, what a nice taste you have in figures of speech!"

"Eh? What's that? Figures of speech? Oh, I'm no scholar, I'm not concerned with elegant language. I'm just a plain fellow—and quite exhausted at the moment."

Mr. Anderson ambled to the window and glanced out. "Once, in your American forests, I watched some men with hounds hunting a bear. The bear was a cub. The little creature got to a tree, which must have seemed to him a sanctuary; he scuffled and scrambled his way up the trunk and out upon a limb. Of course, he shouldn't have done so. He should have stayed hugging the trunk, for the men had only to tear off the limb and down he flopped—and the hounds were upon him."

"Eh? A hunting anecdote?" Mr. Smith mused. "Or perhaps you yourself have a taste in figures of speech. I judge *you* are a scholar, and I must say you're not quite what I expected, from General Arnold's description of you."

Mr. Anderson smiled. "Neither are you quite what I expected. Ah, but that's a trifle, isn't it? You and I scarcely matter."

"No," Mr. Smith said gravely. "General Arnold is the one who matters. And he's a smart man. Very smart. If—now heed me, for I'm only saying *if*—you should be halted anywhere, send for the General and he'll be with you in a trice. In a *trice,* sir!"

"Sacrificing his convenience to my whimsy?"

"Yes, sir! He would be right beside you, explaining who you are."

"His merchant friend from New York City?"

"Exactly. And that's all there'd be to that, sir!" Mr. Smith yawned and chuckled. "But you'll look a scarecrow in my coat. You're not stout enough to fill it out to perfection."

"Hardly." Mr. John Anderson's smile was rueful. "No, I'm hardly stout enough to look very stylish. And that, I fancy, is another trifle."

18

THUNDER IN THE HIGHLANDS

AS GRANNY AFTERWARD REMARKED, THE MYSTERIOUS THUNder of the Hudson Highlands, rolling and billowing behind the blue of a cloudless sky, had never been so loud as on that Saturday morning.

She was seated in her armchair at the window, reading the Bible to Kirby, on a stool beside her. Isaiah, the thirty-third chapter: " 'Woe to thee that spoilest, and thou wast not spoiled; and dealest treacherously, and they dealt not treacherously with thee!' "

"I can't hear you, Granny. All that noise!"

She thrust her work-worn finger between the pages, to mark the place. She took off her spectacles, squinted upward, shook her silvery head.

"Well, it *is* a tumult." She put on her spectacles and read again: " '—when thou shalt cease to spoil, thou shalt be spoiled; and when thou shalt make an end to deal treacherously, they shall deal treacherously with thee.

" 'O Lord, be gracious unto us . . . our salvation also in the time of trouble.' "

Kirby listened, liking Granny's voice almost as much as the sonorous words.

" 'For the Lord is our judge, the Lord is our lawgiver, the Lord is our king; he will save us.' "

The thunder was heard at Robinson's House.

The baby startled up, whimpering, from slumber. Mistress Arnold screamed; and Bolton dropped the saucer of scented powder which she had been brushing into the lady's beautiful hair. In the kitchen Catherine Martin said to Emmeline: "I never *will* get used to it!"

And in the library Colonel Richard Varick and Major David Franks clasped hands.

"So then, if our doubts should be confirmed, we must leave him?" The Colonel paused. "Before it is too late?"

"Yes, on my honor. But still I hope," said Franks, "with all my heart I *hope* they will not be confirmed."

The young man riding the White Plains road heard the thunder. He was alone; Mr. Joshua Smith had turned back after their breakfast together in the village which was named, amusingly, Cat Hill. He had fifteen miles more to go, through alien country. He was not afraid—not that!—but he was wary.

He smiled, wondering what Sir Henry Clinton would say to see him, shorn of the splendid coat of an officer in His Majesty's army. He had retained the nankeen waistcoat and breeches, the white-topped boots; they were such attire as anybody might own. But he felt that he looked absurd in Mr. Smith's claret-colored coat—sizes too large!—with the gold-laced buttons and buttonholes, and the civilian hat, not cocked, but round and low-crowned.

"Like a Yankee squire. Like the General's merchant friend from New York City!"

Sir Henry would surely have disapproved of the costume. Well, he would have been critical of this adventure too, all of it. Sir Henry had never thought that Mr. John Anderson would quit the *Vulture* for a night trip to Joshua Smith's house. Nor had Mr. John Anderson thought so. The negotiations were to have occurred aboard the sloop, within the protection of British banners—and British guns. How and why had things got so confused? What was the excuse for his being here now, like this? The situation was tricky, to say the least!

At Cat Hill, Mr. Smith had warned that there were cowboys abroad this morning.

"Cowboys?"

"Loyalist marauders. They smuggle American cattle—and whatever else they can lay hands on. They may plague you a bit, but they're not dangerous."

"You know that the cowboys *are* Loyalists, Mr. Smith?"

"Oh, yes."

Mr. John Anderson had said nothing more. If the marauders were Loyalists, he need not fear them.

He rode at a trot, appreciating the wiriness and stamina of his horse—the horse which General Arnold had offered with such a lordly gesture. Only once did the horse falter. That was when the thunder rumbled eerily, from heavens which seemed clear and placid. The rider's hand tightened on the bridle. It wouldn't do for him to be thrown, injured or incapacitated in any way, for on his person were documents which would affect vast territory, a kingdom, thousands of human lives.

And how strange this was, if you thought about it!—that a slim youth, with England in his heart and a silly round hat, like a saucepan, on his head, should be for the brief interval in control of destiny.

But perhaps General Benedict Arnold had the same feeling, that *he* was destiny's controller. Mr. John Anderson's mouth curled scornfully. No, he would not bracket himself, even in imagination, with Benedict Arnold; he had no admiration for the General. Indeed, Arnold was, if anything, less admirable than Mr. Smith—who probably was only a doddering old fool, a fussbudget swollen with vanity at being involved in a scheme of a cleverer man's devising. Smith was a person to be despised, a weakling and a pawn.

But Benedict Arnold was something else—and more.

Mr. John Anderson did not know just what to think of Benedict Arnold.

They had been acquainted for a long time. In Philadelphia they often had attended the same parties and balls. And Mistress Arnold, as Miss Peggy Shippen, had been Mr. Anderson's friend. Once he had sketched a crayon portrait of Miss Peggy, and he had asked her to let him be her knight in the grand tournament of the festival celebrating Lord Howe's occupancy of the city.

He had thought then that Miss Peggy was the sweetest and loveliest young lady on earth! He had been just on the brink of telling her so, of declaring his feeling for her. Then somehow, he hadn't; and soon thereafter she had married Benedict Arnold. Her marriage had made everything different, and Mr. John Anderson had decided that she must be another sort of woman entirely from what he had believed, a woman with temperament and traits to match those of her husband—and therefore scarcely lovely at all. Mr John Anderson had almost forgotten the enchanting Miss Peggy. He knew now that she had not been the girl for him.

The horse trotted down Hardscrabble Road, past Chappaqua. At Pleasantville, a boy was pumping water from a well. Mr. John Anderson slackened. "Am I on the way to White Plains, lad?"

"That you are, sir. But the cowboys are skirmishing ahead. You'd best branch off here to the Tarrytown pike."

The rider nodded, and veered into the Tarrytown pike. He went several miles, to a bridge—

And just then the thunder came again, suddenly with such a prodigious, deafening clamor that the horse shuddered from neck to tail, and pranced on hind legs, and whinnied.

"Whoa! Softly! Easy a while!" Mr. John Anderson reined in.

It was just as well. He would have had to stop, anyway; for squirming out from under the bridge were three stalwart men, unshaven and ragged, with muskets in their hands.

They swarmed up, snatching at the bridle. "Get down, traveler."

Mr. John Anderson leaped to the ground. He was smiling. "You may lower your firelocks, gentlemen. They are too near my breast. I am of your politics."

They looked blankly at him and one of them said: "What politics is that?"

His smile did not waver. "You are cowboys, aren't you?"

"No. We're skinners."

"Skinners?" The word was new to Mr. John Anderson; he did not know what it meant. "Skinners?" His voice had a rising inflection. "You are—not Loyalists?"

"We're not. An' no more are you, if you know what's good for you!"

"Just as I thought." But in the instant, the traveler's viewpoint, his manner and his whole world had altered. "Well, gentlemen, we are of the identical persuasion. I am a merchant from New York, summoned to the Highlands on a business mission with General Arnold. You know him?"

"O' course," said the skinners' leader.

"I have passes from the General here." Mr. John Anderson dug them out of his pocket. He also extracted his gold watch, which he dangled conspicuously on its thick chain.

They swarmed up, snatching at the bridle

"I beg you to make haste in examining the passes, for I must get along to White Plains. I cannot afford to be detained."

"There are many bad people on the road these days," said the man who was holding the horse.

"No doubt, no doubt! But I am not one of them."

The leader had been reading the slips of paper, spelling out the words, puzzling over them. "They look all right," he said slowly. "Hi! ain't that a crest on the watch? Ain't it a British crest?"

"Not at all! My name is John Anderson." He pocketed the watch, which had not served its purpose. "I am an American, a merchant—"

"We'll have to search him." The chief skinner folded the papers and flung them aside. "Come, into the bushes with him and off with his clothes!"

"But, gentlemen!"

"Are you scared to be searched?"

"No, I am not!"

"Then let's be at it, mates!"

They dragged him behind the clump of hazel bushes and stripped off his claret-colored coat, his nankeen breeches, his boots.

"Well, are you convinced?" He stood in his underwear, and dignity did not forsake him.

They were inspecting the inside of the round hat, running fingers down into the toes of the boots. Nothing, nothing.

"But he's still got his stockings on!"

"Now, gentlemen, I protest!"

"His stockings! Take 'em off!"

Without more ado, the stockings were pulled off. Two thin packets of documents fell out. The chief skinner stooped and plucked them up. As he read them, his mouth moved with each syllable—and there was a hush profound as death.

Then, his voice queer and hoarse, the skinner said: "Why, mates, he's a spy! That's what he is—*a spy!*"

"Nonsense!" The young man laughed.

"It says here—"

"You simply interpret it in the wrong light. Gentlemen, I am a reasonable chap and I feel sure you also are reasonable. We will talk over this matter quite reasonably. You are not soldiers but citizens, with a living to earn by sweat and toil. Tell me, who are you?"

"I'm John Paulding of North Salem," said the chief skinner. "This is Isaac Van Wart. T'other one is David Williams of Tarrytown."

"Very good. Now, Paulding and Van Wart and Williams, you and I will bargain and not quarrel. I must go on. To do so is worth a great deal to me. What is your price?"

"Will you give us your horse—saddle, bridle and all?" queried Paulding.

"Yes, I will."

"And the watch?"

"That, too."

"And one hundred guineas?" said Van Wart.

"One hundred guineas—each." He was cool and collected, bargaining. "The money will be delivered to any spot you direct."

"And what more?" asked Williams.

"More? Well, any amount of dry goods, such as cloth, either wool or silk, equal portions to the three of you. Or flour, wine, sugar."

"Ten thousand guineas would be nearer the price!" ejaculated Paulding.

"Ten thousand? That is an exorbitant sum. But—"

"Even then I wouldn't let you go!" Paulding seemed to

be remembering something. "We're patriots, we are! Volunteer militiamen! Whatever property is on a captured enemy we can claim as a prize—an' so the law says! Horse, saddle, watch, they're ours. But the promises you may keep, stranger! *And we will not let you go!*" He shoved his captive rudely. "How dare you try to bribe us? Put on your clothes again. We're taking you to North Castle."

"And where is that?"

"You'll know all in good time. Major Tallmadge is there. You'll be turned over to him." Paulding strode into the road and mounted the horse. "Up here with me, Williams. Van Wart can walk with him . . . Hi! what *is* your name?"

"I have told you. Anderson." Very slowly he was dressing himself, stamping into the boots, shrugging into the detested silk coat which did not fit him.

"Your *real* name?"

"And where you've played your spying game?" cried Van Wart. "All about you?"

"I will tell Major Tallmadge, at North Castle, whatever is necessary. He will liberate me—and perhaps apologize."

"Ho!" croaked Paulding derisively. "You'll tell us."

"I think not. No, you are mistaken. In asking questions, you but waste your breath." He donned the hat and flipped the brim with his thumb. "Shall we proceed?"

Major Tallmadge was not on duty at North Castle that day. He had gone to White Plains; and when Paulding, his friends and the captive went into the small logs-and-stone building which served as headquarters for the American troops there, it was to find Lieutenant-colonel Jameson in command.

Though Jameson's rank was superior, he was an officer of far less experience than Major Tallmadge—and now he was frankly perplexed. He bent over the table on which the papers were spread.

"Mr. John Anderson? Yes, yes! I remember that General Arnold wrote Major Tallmadge to expect you. Colonel Sheldon had a letter, too. And your passes seem to be in order. They are all in General Arnold's hand. You are returning to New York?"

"I am, sir. I have a mercantile establishment in New York."

"But these other documents? They are also in the General's hand, though not signed by him. I confess I do not understand them."

Frowning, Jameson studied the documents.

One was a statement of the West Point artillery orders, showing the disposition to be made of the corps, in case of an alarm. (It would be of immeasurable assistance to any enemy who planned to invade the fortress!) A second was an estimate of the forces at West Point and all its dependent garrisons, numbering the men required to defend the works of the main fortress and those smaller outposts in the hills and up and down the river. There was a list of the American cannon, saying where each was located; and with this was a detailed description of the structure of the forts, with special mention of such walls as were weakened. (What interesting reading to an enemy who might wish to storm those walls!) The fifth document was a copy of the report of a council of war held recently by General Washington, at which the commander-in-chief had set forth starkly the sorry condition of his army, its gloomy prospects as well as its indomitably gallant hopes—what the colonists had accomplished in their long struggle and what they must yet accomplish before ultimate victory should be won. (How enlightening to an enemy, who with this information would know just where and when that victory could be forestalled!)

Jameson was quite baffled, studying, wagging his head, looking up. "Mr. Anderson, I think I must send you back to General Arnold. I really do."

"Very well, sir. I should prefer, of course, to continue my journey, but—I wish you to be satisfied of my identity."

"I cannot see how you could be in possession of these documents—unless you have stolen them. But I am not justified in charging you with theft, since General Arnold said you would be coming this way."

"I feel sure that it will all be straightened out when I have been sent back to the General."

"You will have a guard; and I shall pen a few lines to General Arnold telling him that the documents are of a very dangerous tendency."

"Anything you say, sir."

"You had better start for West Point at once."

Here Paulding and his friends interrupted. What about them? Were they not to be rewarded for their vigilance? What kind of treatment was this, for patriotic men? If this Mr. John Anderson wasn't a spy—well, he might just as well have been, for all the skinners knew!

Mr. John Anderson smiled. "I have already told you that the booty is yours. Horse, saddle, bridle, watch and chain—divide them between you."

When the New York merchant had gone, under guard, toward West Point, Lieutenant-colonel Jameson dispatched the documents to General Washington who, he knew, was on his way back from Hartford and must now be in the vicinity of Peekskill. The courier was told to hurry. Later in the day, Jameson related the whole puzzling story to Major Tallmadge, returned to North Castle from scouting duty to the south.

"And you did not hold that man!" Tallmadge was shocked. "Why he was a spy!"

"Oh, no, Major!"

"Certainly he was a spy! Paulding and the skinners knew it. Why not you?"

"But the *writing?* It was General Arnold's!"

"I do not care one fig about the writing!" Major Tallmadge was wrathful. "With that information the British could wreck us, ruin our cause, paralyze our army, end our resistance! If Benedict Arnold wrote those documents, he is linked in a conspiracy!"

"No, Major!"

"I say *yes!*" roared Tallmadge. "A traitorous conspiracy, sir! And you released that man and he has fled into the open where he can never be recaptured!"

"The guard—"

"What if he gets away from the guard?"

"I will send after him, sir!" Jameson was terribly regretful, quaking before the Major's ire. "I will have him seized and brought here!"

The fastest horse in the stable bore the sergeant who galloped after Mr. John Anderson and his guard. They were overtaken near Peekskill, hustled back to North Castle, into the presence of the thoroughly dismayed Jameson and the grim-jawed Major Tallmadge.

"We are transferring you to the jail at Lower Salem," said Tallmadge, without ceremony. "The papers you carried, all of them, have been forwarded to General Washington."

Mr. John Anderson hesitated. "You say they *have been* forwarded?"

"Yes. Several hours ago."

"Then I myself shall write to His Excellency."

"That would be most irregular!"

"No, I do not think so." He was silent a moment. "I shall tell General Washington the truth."

"Which is—"

"That I am Major John André, adjutant general of the British army.

"Ah!" Major Tallmadge shot a withering look at Lieutenant-colonel Jameson.

"That I came within the American lines to meet someone who was to give me military intelligence—and that I was betrayed into masquerading as a spy, disguised—and vilely! within your posts." He drew himself to full height. "But I will be branded with nothing dishonorable. I have no motive save the service of my king. I was involuntarily an imposter."

In the cell at Lower Salem, Major André (erstwhile a merchant from New York) composed his letter and next morning procured a messenger to take it to General Washington. At about the same time, Lieutenant-colonel Jameson exercised what seemed a genius for blundering by speeding a messenger to General Arnold at Robinson's House with a lengthy account of the unfathomable happening.

Though neither messenger realized it, they were engaged in a race. Would Washington be first to learn that treason had been revealed—or would Benedict Arnold?

Much depended upon that!

19

FATEFUL MORNING

EMMELINE BALANCED THE BREAKFAST TRAY VERY CAREFULLY as she went up the stairs. Earlier this Monday morning she had dropped and broken a plate. She didn't want to do so again! Like everyone else at Robinson's House, Emmeline was feeling nervous and jumpy today. She thought it was because General Washington and his staff were coming. The great man had been expected on Sunday, but then he had notified General Arnold that he was delayed and would lodge overnight in Fishkill. Now the preparations to receive him were under way.

It seemed strange to Emmeline that, with the household so disorganized, Mistress Arnold should have to take her breakfast in bed. But there!—as Catherine Martin often said—you couldn't account for the whims of such people. You just had to humor them.

The weather was cool and rather dreary, and Emmeline was unhappily aware, as she always was of late, of the tension which prevailed within these walls. It did not subside, but grew. Peace was what Emmeline liked, and was accustomed to, at home. But here peace was a rarity, and more and more it was disspelled by harrowing scenes.

The week-end had been trying, and Emmeline was inclined to blame the Joshua Smiths for that. They had come again on Saturday, both Mr. and Mistress Smith; and their visit had upset Colonel Varick so badly that he had been very discourteous again. That night, at the dinner table, Colonel Varick had quite lost control of his temper—and all about the butter, or the shortage of butter! A trifling thing, at most. But in these times you never could tell what trifle would start an argument.

Emmeline had just served the salt fish, when Mistress Arnold saw there was not enough butter. She had called for a fresh dish of it.

"I am sorry, ma'am," Emmeline had said (and she was honestly sorry!), "but we have no more."

General Arnold had glanced up then. "Bless me! I had forgot the olive oil I bought in Philadelphia. It will do well with the fish. Excuse me, and I will fetch it."

He had gone himself down cellar, for the olive oil was kept in that room to which only he had the key.

When he got it, he had waited in the kitchen while Catherine Martin filled the crystal cruet, and then he had taken the cruet to the table.

"We must savor it," he had said, with a smile for his guests. "Olive oil now sells for eighty dollars a pint."

"You mean in continental money?" said Mr. Smith. "That would be about the equivalent of eighty pence in English coin. The American dollar has so little value."

At that Colonel Varick had laid down his fork. "There is nothing the matter with the American dollar. It is sound."

"Oh, now, Colonel!" Mr. Smith remonstrated.

"I resent your disparaging comment upon everything American. For Americans to talk of the small value of their money is unseemly." He looked at Major Franks. "Do you agree, sir?"

"Yes," said Major Franks. "Such talk is not for patriots."

"Well, well," said Mr. Smith, "I do really find it very difficult to get on with you, Colonel. I suppose my language is at fault. I am not a scholar—"

"The question is," said Colonel Varick bluntly, "are you an American?"

The pause following this speech was long and dramatic. As if he could not believe his ears, General Arnold glared at his secretary.

"Colonel Varick, you will beg Mr. Smith's pardon."

"For a question which requires so simple an answer? No, sir."

"Oh, dear!" Mistress Smith had wailed, rising from her chair. "*Must* we have such dissension?"

And Mistress Arnold had exclaimed: "I insist that the subject be changed!" And she had changed it, quickly and tactfully.

Afterward Emmeline had heard General Arnold's voice, raging at Colonel Varick. The two men, with Major Franks, were closeted in Colonel Varick's chamber.

"You wilfully sought to affront Mr. Smith!"

"No, sir. But I did not object to affronting him, when the occasion offered."

"Let me tell you, Varick, that if I asked the devil to dine with me, the gentlemen of my family would have to be civil to him!"

"The devil is not the worst companion I can think of. If Smith hadn't been at your table, I should have aimed the wine bottle at his pompous bald head! I shall behave toward him as I see fit, sir. He is an unmitigated rascal."

Major Franks' voice had been calmer. "I think, General Arnold, that the Colonel is right in this instance. Smith *is* a rascal—and he may even be a spy. No friend of yours would ever sanction your intimacy with him."

There was a silence, and then General Arnold said, less stridently: "I am always to be advised by the gentlemen of my family. But remember, Varick—and you also, Franks— I will not be *dictated to* by them! I have as much prudence as either of you, and better judgment. But what folly for us to differ so violently about Joshua Smith! I shall not be going to his house in the future. Nor will I be seen with him in company."

And with that assertion, the dissension and the differing had ceased, for soon the Smiths had left, Major Franks had ridden off to Newburgh on an errand; and Colonel Varick had gone to bed to nurse a sore throat.

Emmeline thought it might be the sore throat which had irritated Colonel Varick, as much as had the Joshua Smiths. She fixed a flaxseed poultice for him and a mug of hot toddy which he drank gratefully. But he was still in bed, his thin face very red, as if he had a fever. He would not be up to greet General Washington or General Lafayette or the members of their staffs.

Emmeline knocked timidly on Mistress Arnold's door and, at a word from within, she entered. The curtains were down, but the lady was awake, sitting up in bed, her head against a pile of ruffled pillows. The towering structure of her hair was covered with a silk net, and she had no rouge on her lips or cheeks. Even so, and in the cold gray morning light, when Emmeline had raised the curtains, Mistress Arnold looked very pretty, fragile as a flower, her neck and arms milk-white, her eyes big and liquid.

Emmeline set the tray on the bureau and from the closet got a lacy wrapper which she threw around Mistress Arnold's shoulders.

"I hope you rested well, ma'am."

"I never rest well. What day is this?"

"Monday, September twenty-fifth. General Washington is coming."

"I wish he wouldn't," said Mistress Arnold pettishly. "I wish the day was over."

Emmeline put the tray before Mistress Arnold, and a spoon clattered to the floor.

"Oh, you awkward, clumsy girl!"

"Forgive me, ma'am. But it was only a spoon."

"It's always *something*," cried Mistress Arnold. "Oh, why do you torture me with your clumsiness when I have so much to endure? I am the most wretched person alive!"

Emmeline said nothing, but she gazed at the lady and wondered at her wretchedness. What, actually, had she to endure? In the ten days since her arrival at Robinson's House, Mistress Arnold had not, to Emmeline's knowledge, turned her hand. She did not even tend her own baby; she never bathed or fed him, never cuddled or rocked or played with him. From morning till night she was waited upon, indulged, pampered, by a doting husband, two young officers who adored her and several servants hired expressly to run their legs off for her whenever she spoke. Emmeline herself had been up with the dawn, cleaning, scouring, polishing, helping Catherine Martin bake cakes and pies and stuff a goose—and her tasks were just begun. There would be twelve more hours of such effort before she could stretch out on her narrow cot up under the eaves.

Emmeline's eyes must have had a mildly accusing gleam, for Mistress Arnold fidgeted.

"You *are* awkward and uncouth, don't deny it."

"I'm not denying it, ma'am."

"But I daresay it's because you've no training. I'll not be too hard on you. Do you see that bracelet on the dressing-table? Take it—and after this, try to be more mannerly!"

Emmeline looked toward the dressing-table, and the bracelet there. It was a bauble of silver with green and yellow glass settings which Mistress Arnold often wore on her beautiful wrist.

"I do not think I have been unmannerly, ma'am," said Emmeline clearly. "And I do not want the bracelet."

Not for worlds would she have touched it!

As she went out of the room she was thinking of another morning—and Mr. Rawlins. "Why, she was treating me just as General Arnold did the fisherman! An insult first, which wasn't deserved—and then an expensive gift to cure our hurt feelings! But *I* will not be treated so!"

Downstairs, she said to Catherine Martin: "I have made up my mind that I don't like Mistress Arnold. I don't like her at all! She is just *too* spoiled."

"Hush!" Catherine pushed her butterfly bow askew and rubbed her forehead. Catherine was tired yet brisk. "This is no time for chattering. It's nine o'clock and Colonel Alexander Hamilton is here to say that General Washington will be late, and the meal must go on without him. That means *two* breakfasts—one now, and another, tasty and piping hot, in perhaps an hour. You baste the fowl, Emmeline. Then everything will be in readiness."

Scarcely had the officers seated themselves in the diningroom when a horseman dashed up to the veranda of Robinson's House and asked for General Arnold. The host murmured apologies and got up from his place at the head of the table. He went out into the hall.

"A letter for you, sir, from Lieutenant-colonel Jameson at North Castle. And he said to tell you that John Anderson has been taken prisoner."

"*What!*" Arnold seemed to reel. Slowly the blood drained from his swarthy face.

"It's all in the letter, sir; but I was to tell you, also. Mr. John Anderson—the papers discovered on him have been forwarded to General Washington."

Arnold did not reply immediately. Beads of perspiration appeared on his pallid brow. Then he said hoarsely: "Very well. Begone! *Begone,* you imbecile!"

The messenger turned and fled.

After a minute, Arnold climbed the stairs, jerkily, as if his lamed leg annoyed him. He went along the upper corridor and into Mistress Arnold's chamber and shut the door.

Within another minute a lean young courier cantered to Robinson's House, to inform Major Franks, who was called from the table, that General Washington was approaching.

"His Excellency is just around the bend in the road!"

Major Franks saluted, and went upstairs; at Mistress Arnold's door he halted. "Sir, General Washington is near."

Arnold opened the door a little way and peered out at Franks. "Major, I am in somewhat of a dilemma."

"Can I do anything, sir?"

"Yes. Receive His Excellency with all courtesies and see that he has his meal. Tell him I've had to go to West Point, but I'll return shortly—in thirty or sixty minutes. If a horse is saddled, I'll ride to the dock."

"General Washington's courier has a horse."

"Good!" Arnold reached behind him and caught up a black coat and his hat.

"I hope it's not serious trouble at the fort, sir."

"Oh, no! Well, Franks, you do the honors for me."

Major Franks went downstairs. He thought (but he wasn't sure) that Mistress Arnold had been sobbing as the General spoke.

Arnold waited until Franks was in the dining room. Then he came out into the corridor, tiptoed to the rear stairs and down, and through the kitchen.

"Well, I never!" Catherine Martin said. "What is it, sir?"

But he did not so much as glance at Catherine. He went into the yard where the courier's horse was standing. He swung up into the saddle and slapped the horse on the flank.

Emmeline, emerging from the dining room, found Catherine at the window.

"There he goes, fast as greased lightning!"

"Who goes?"

"The master of Robinson's House."

Emmeline looked over Catherine's shoulder. "Whose horse is that?"

"The courier's. I told the boy to wash his hands at the pump and I'd give him a bite to eat. I told him you'd likely give him a kiss."

"Why, Catherine!" Emmeline was mortified. "How dreadful of you!" But just then the courier came from the pump. *"It's Jed!"* Emmeline cried joyfully, and ran to give him the kiss.

20

"WHOM CAN WE TRUST NOW?"

WHAT WAS HAPPENING AT ROBINSON'S HOUSE?

Afterward, looking back, Emmeline and Jed could piece together the incidents, bit by bit, as you would fit the segments of a picture puzzle, and realize that between them, they had a better-than-average knowledge of an event of world-wide portent. But at the time they knew only bewilderment and in their few moments of conversation, snatched from duties, they could merely say to each other:

"What *is* it? What is happening?"

An astonishing day, moving with a rapidity that made you sick and giddy! . . .

No sooner had Emmeline rushed out into the yard to embrace her brother than Catherine Martin was signaling from the window. General Washington was in sight! Once more the table was readied and all the best portions of food (which Catherine had kept hot) were ladled into cups and dishes. Emmeline was to serve His Excellency's meal. She was breathless with anticipation.

She had never before seen General Washington; but she thought, as he came into the dining room, that she would have known him anywhere. He was not like other men. Courage and decision were in his every gesture, repose in every feature of his fine countenance. You felt, seeing him, not just a firmness in him but in yourself, too, in everything —an assurance that human existence had purpose, that right must triumph in the world of men. His uniform was, as always, immaculate, his complexion ruddy; his eyes were blue.

"And I'm glad," thought Emmeline, "he has his hair powdered today. His face is just the sort to set off powdered hair!"

Lafayette and several other officers sat at the table with Washington; they told him that General Arnold had been called to West Point.

"I shall go to the fort and meet General Arnold. You will please remain here, Colonel Hamilton, lest there be communications directed to me at this place."

"I believe," said Hamilton, "it has been arranged that we are all to dine with Mistress Arnold at four this afternoon."

Washington smiled. "You younger men will like that! And I, also. I have known Mistress Arnold since she was a little child. My compliments to her, Colonel Hamilton, and say that I shall be prompt for the dinner . . . Well, I shall go down to Beverley Dock and unearth a barge for my passage across the Hudson. I presume General Arnold will have taken his own boat. He is probably preparing to salute us with a great burst of cannon!"

Had Washington not departed just then, he would have heard the thin, high shrieking which broke forth in Robinson's House a moment later. Everyone there heard it, an uncanny, blood-curdling noise. Everyone was transfixed, wondering what it could be. The next moment brought an explanation. Now Bolton, Mistress Arnold's maid, was at the top of the stairs, leaning over, her cry even louder than the shrieking.

"My lady's ill. Oh, she is very ill! Help me!"

Major Franks was first to respond. He was up the steps in a bound, with Catherine and Emmeline at his heels. While they were yet in the corridor, Colonel Varick stumbled from his room and followed them. His hair was disheveled and he was throwing on his clothes as he ran. Colonel Hamilton, as a stranger here, followed more slowly, and behind him were four soldiers, Jed Drake among them, who had been somewhere on the premises and had come inside at the cry for help. To one of these men, Colonel Hamilton said:

"Dr. Eustis, His Excellency's physician, is in the neighborhood, at Dwight's cottage a mile south. Get him."

As Major Franks opened the door of Mistress Arnold's room, the lady was to be seen, standing in the center of the floor. She was in her lacy nightgown, but the net was off her hair and it had been elaborately dressed. She had the baby in her arms; her face was white as chalk and tears streamed from her eyes, as from her lips issued the frenzied shrieking.

"Mistress Arnold!" said Major Franks, and he went to her and grasped her elbow. "My dear lady—"

She shook off his hand. "Where—where is Colonel Varick?" she gasped.

"Here!" The Colonel was pushing past everyone else; he was beside her. "What is it, madam? What's the matter?"

Mistress Arnold clutched at his sleeve. "Oh, Colonel Varick, have you ordered my little baby to be killed?"

"Why, madam!"

"Yes! Yes, you have! Oh, how cruel you are to me! How I am persecuted!"

"But, Mistress Arnold!" Colonel Varick was horrified. "This is madness! I have not ordered any such thing!"

With a blood-curdling scream, she sank at his feet. "I pray you, do not kill my innocent baby!" Then she was abruptly still, except for the wheezing of her labored breathing.

Colonel Varick bent and tried to raise her. No man was ever more distressed than he; and the others came quickly to relieve him. Bolton took the baby and laid him in his crib. Major Franks assisted the Colonel in lifting Mistress Arnold from the floor to her bed; and Catherine Martin fetched a pitcher of water from the washstand, dipped a towel into the water and sponged the lady's tear-stained cheeks.

"She is out of her head," whispered Major Franks.

"Raving," said Colonel Varick. "Distracted."

"Hysterics," pronounced Catherine, dipping the towel again, squeezing it and applying the cold linen surface vigorously to Mistress Arnold's face. "Hysterics. I've often seen her like this. There's no need to worry too much. When the doctor comes, he'll give her something."

"The doctor is on his way," said Colonel Hamilton, from the door. "May I suggest that we leave her, now that she has been quieted? She will be the better for rest."

"A good suggestion, sir," said Catherine. "Bolton, you move the baby's crib into your own chamber. That poor little mite should be protected! What if his mother had dropped him while she was ranting so? The baby's in more danger from Mistress Arnold than from Colonel Varick—though no meaning should be attached to anything she said, for she doesn't know what she's saying! I'll go downstairs and await the doctor, and you gentlemen will probably want to come down, too. But you, Emmeline, stay up here and watch for signs of the hysterics returning."

They were all grateful for Catherine's commonsense, and they shifted about to do her bidding. But Colonel Varick said that he would stay, also. It was evident that he was very anxious and overwrought himself.

"I think we should send for General Arnold!"

"No," said Major Franks. "He will be here within the hour, anyway."

When the others had withdrawn, a strained silence settled over the room where Emmeline and Colonel Varick were left with Mistress Arnold. She seemed to have fallen into a fitful sleep, disturbed by groans and mutterings. Emmeline kept the cold wet towel on her forehead, and the Colonel, looking quite miserable, sat beside the bed.

Occasionally Mistress Arnold would open her eyes and stare at Colonel Varick.

"I am alone. Alone! I have no friends here!"

"My dear lady, you are not alone. You do have friends. You have Major Franks and me, and your husband will soon be coming."

"No, General Arnold has gone. He will never return."

"He is at West Point. He will be back at any minute. I swear it!"

"No, he has gone *forever*. I shall never see my husband again."

Then Mistress Arnold would lapse into troubled slumber, only to rouse presently and repeat her assertions that she was alone and had no friends, that General Arnold had gone, never to return to Robinson's House.

"I could almost believe," whispered Colonel Varick, glancing at Emmeline, "that there is something in it. What *did* the General say, Emmeline, when he rode away?"

"Nothing to me, sir, of course. And not a word to Catherine. But he spoke with both Mistress Arnold and Major Franks; and Major Franks told General Washington what we all know, that General Arnold had gone only to West Point for the hour."

Then, after a long time, the doctor came and administered a draft of medicine; and Mistress Arnold relaxed into a deeper sleep.

"Let us leave her," said the doctor. "She will sleep while the effects of the potion last, and when she wakes she will be herself and call for someone. And her husband will be able to calm her."

At noon the barge which carried General Washington moored at Beverley Dock, and His Excellency stepped ashore. The visit to West Point had been an odd one. Not only had no salute of cannon been fired when Washington's barge was sighted, but he had alighted without any notice at all being paid him. As he went up the bluff from the landing-stage, he encountered Colonel Lamb, second in command, strolling down toward the river, his dress and manner casual.

Seeing Washington, Colonel Lamb stopped and, amazed, snapped to attention. In spite of his military discipline, Colonel Lamb blurted: "Your Excellency! Why, where have you come from?"

"Announce me to General Arnold, sir."

"But the General is not here, Your Excellency."

"Not here?"

"He has not been at West Point these two days, nor have I heard from him."

"Colonel Lamb," Washington said, after a pause, "I have intended to inspect the works this morning and I shall do so, whether or not your superior officer is present."

That inspection consumed the forenoon; Colonel Lamb had been dutiful and efficient—and General Arnold had not appeared.

Now, again on the Hudson's west bank, Washington saw Colonel Hamilton hurrying along the path toward him.

"Sir, there is something I must—must show you." Hamilton could not conceal his agitation. "A messenger has come from North Castle with a packet of documents taken from the person of a suspected spy—and a letter to you from the spy himself."

"This is extraordinary."

"You should have had these papers yesterday." Hamilton

frowned. "But Jameson's messenger missed our party when we took the upper road out of Danbury."

"Is General Arnold at the house, Hamilton?"

"He is not. And no word of him. Except—"

"Yes. Go on."

"The report may be false, sir. But Dr. Eustis said that he was told that Arnold's barge was being towed down the river toward Verplanck's Point. That was several hours ago."

"You will go at once to Verplanck's Point, Hamilton. You will intercept General Arnold there and bring him back immediately."

"I will, sir."

As Washington proceeded to Robinson's House there was no alteration in his erect bearing, but his blue eyes were clouded with something like fear. He went into the library where General Knox and General Lafayette were standing, very silently. On the table were the documents from North Castle.

Washington read them, all of them, and the letter signed with the name of Major John André of the British army.

"Gentlemen," he said, slowly, "this is treachery."

"But *whose?*" Lafayette cried in a voice of agony.

"Benedict Arnold's treachery. Your friend and mine." Washington's face was so grave, so infinitely sad that the hearts of all who heard him were stirred with pity.

"Gentlemen," Washington said, looking about him, *"whom can we trust now?"*

21

TRAITOR UNMASKED

JED DRAKE WAS ONE OF THE SOLDIERS WHO GALLOPED WITH Colonel Alexander Hamilton to Verplanck's Point. But the little band of horsemen reached there only to learn that General Arnold's barge had passed the dock long before noon. A sentry at the river's edge had hailed it. General Arnold had ignored the waving banner and forged on southward.

The sentry said that the eight bargemen had plied their oars with the greatest zeal, and the current was strongly with them. At such a rate of speed, the boat must now be far down the Hudson.

"I should think," remarked Jed to the comrade nearest him, "that the bargemen would have refused to obey General Arnold. Surely they must have known!"

"No, Drake," said the comrade, who was older than Jed, a veteran in years and experience. "The bargemen could not have known what the scoundrel was up to. But if they did—why, perhaps they rowed in fear of their lives, with a pistol leveled at their heads!"

As Colonel Hamilton, sick with disappointment, was turning away from the Verplanck's dock, he spied through his glass a small boat coming up the river. There was a square white flag floating from a pole at the stern. It was a flag of truce, and the men in the boat were seen, as they came closer, to be wearing British uniforms.

Colonel Hamilton waited. The boat nosed alongside the

dock and a man scrambled out of it and handed Hamilton two letters.

"These are for General Washington. Will you have them delivered to him? He is at Robinson's House."

"I will deliver them," Hamilton said. "Where are you from?"

"His Majesty's armed sloop, the *Vulture*, lying about six miles below."

Colonel Hamilton glanced at the letters. One was addressed in General Arnold's writing.

"Is General Arnold aboard the *Vulture?*"

"Yes, he is. Boarded her soon after twelve o'clock. His bargemen were put in irons, as prisoners of war."

Colonel Hamilton sighed. Mounting his horse, he beckoned to his soldiers and started once more for Robinson's House.

Meanwhile, back there, in her luxurious bedchamber, Mistress Arnold had wakened. She seemed less distracted, yet she demanded to see Colonel Varick, and to him and to Major Franks and to Dr. Eustis she said over and over again that she had been deserted, that her husband had gone forever.

In the corridor, Varick and Franks conferred privately.

"It is delusion!" said Major Franks. "Unless—"

"You are thinking precisely what I'm thinking. Unless he *has* gone forever—gone to the *enemy*."

"He could not be so base, Varick! No man could! I beg you not to mention such a possibility, not to a soul."

"The doctor already has mentioned it. He insisted that General Arnold be summoned, and when I told him that everything was being done that could be done to locate him, Dr. Eustis said perhaps Mistress Arnold has a glimmering of the true state of affairs."

"I shall not believe it! Not without proof!"

Varick ran his fingers through his sandy locks. "I have suspected him of many things. Never of this."

"Your hand is trembling, Varick," said Major Franks. "You have a fever and should not be about. Go to your room and lie down."

"No, I cannot. Peggy—Mistress Arnold—might call for me. She wants to speak with General Washington. If you will ask him to come, I'll attend him to the bedside."

Major Franks looked dubious, but he went downstairs to the library where Washington was pacing the hearth-rug, thinking, planning, trying to untangle the knots of treachery and intrigue which had been so cunningly woven.

To what limits did the plot extend? What men, and how many, were involved? How could he prevent the tragic consequences? These were the problems which the commander-in-chief weighed. He had concluded that nothing was to be gained by attempting to gloss over this terrible occurrence. No, everyone must know; he must consult with all his generals, must test each one and determine whether there were others who had conspired with Benedict Arnold, whether any had been lax or remiss, or had succumbed (as Arnold must have) to temptation or bribery. He had sent messages by courier to them all.

His orders were for the entire division to strike camp, wherever the regiments were, and be on the march, to unite in a single vast body at King's Ferry. He could visualize the consternation in the camps when Arnold's story should become known, how the news would creep from tent to tent, and officers, their voices shocked and suppressed, would issue commands to turn out, to saddle horses and parade. It would be midnight, perhaps—for the couriers had great distances to ride—midnight, darkness, and no drums beaten, no music of the fifes, just the silent, sorrowful, frightened activity, the feeling everywhere of suspense, of doom.

Because the British might attack.

Who knew to what lengths the information contained in those documents might have penetrated? Who had seen them? Who knew now the weaknesses of the American army, where it might most successfully be attacked? Perhaps the enemy was poised for one gigantic battle, one blow which might destroy all that free men had so long fought for. Perhaps this meant the final chapter of the war—and a chapter of defeat through betrayal.

Washington had sent to Lower Salem for Major John André. The prisoner would be brought here tonight, to Robinson's House, where Washington could see and examine him. What was he like? His letter had been manly, straightforward; though he was an enemy and had unquestionably been engaged as a spy, he seemed also, from his letter, to be a man of honor, the victim of circumstances.

"I must have André's recital," Washington had declared. "Bring him to me."

The squad of soldiers detailed for this responsibility had set off through rain which fell lightly at first, and then in a chill downpour.

The library gradually grew duskier. A young girl came in with flaming candles and placed them about on the mantel and in the corners. She was the same girl, with her hair shining in flaxen braids, who had served His Excellency's breakfast, and he acknowledged with a smile her respectful curtsy. He went to the window and peered out, wondering if, possibly, Colonel Hamilton might have intercepted Arnold at Verplanck's. But there was small chance of that!

Washington was at the window when Major Franks came with the request that he speak with Mistress Arnold.

"She is in a desperate mood, sir."

"I will speak with her, certainly."

The interview was distressing. Washington stood with Colonel Varick beside the bed, while Major Franks, Dr. Eustis, and Bolton grouped in the background.

"Madam," Colonel Varick said, "here is His Excellency."

She looked up, blankly. "That is not he!"

Washington took her hand. "Believe me, dear lady."

"You are just another person to torture me, now that I am friendless and deserted."

"You will not be tortured, Mistress Arnold."

"What have you done with my husband? You have spirited him away!" She began to weep bitterly. "My husband has gone from me forever, and I shall be made to suffer."

"Oh, no! I should never permit the innocent to suffer for the sins of the guilty. We all have nothing but compassion for you."

As her weeping continued, General Washington went out into the corridor.

"Poor lady!" His face was warm with sympathy. "Poor, unhappy lady!"

But downstairs, in the kitchen, Catherine Martin was saying to Emmeline: "Those hysterics are very convenient."

"Why, Catherine!" Emmeline exclaimed. "What do you mean?"

"Nothing. Nothing, only that a pretty woman can twist the men around her little finger like so much wax."

"Then you don't think—"

"No, I don't think. I'm a servant and not supposed to think. But remember, Emmeline, I've known Mistress Arnold for several years—and I've always said she might have been a wonderful actress."

Now Colonel Hamilton had returned to Robinson's House. He gave the letters he carried to General Washington. In the one which had been addressed by General Arnold's hand was an enclosure for his wife. She was, of course, much too ill to read it, so Major Franks took it and put it aside.

Washington perused the long letter Arnold had written to him. It was not a plea for pardon or even for understanding, but a brazen, boastful admission that, by connivance with Sir Henry Clinton and Major John André, he had hoped to cause the surrender of West Point and the Highland fortresses to the British—and so to end a war which he considered futile. In this (as always, his life long, he said) he had been guided by his great love for his country; and whatever the world might think of his conduct, he had no qualms of remorse.

He asked no favors for himself and hoped for none, having too often felt his country's ingratitude. But he would ask that Mistress Arnold not be insulted or injured. "She is as good and innocent as an angel," he said, "and is incapable of doing wrong." He begged that she be allowed to go to her friends in Philadelphia, or to join him, as she might choose.

And there was a postscript: Varick and Franks, as well as Joshua Smith, Esquire, were not to be suspected of participation in the plot.

The other letter delivered by Colonel Hamilton was also dated from the *Vulture*. Colonel Beverley Robinson had just learned of Major André's capture and was indignantly demanding his instant release.

"Major André," wrote Robinson, "cannot be detained by you . . . Every step Major André took was by the advice and direction of General Arnold, even that of taking a feigned name, and of course he is not liable to censure for it."

Washington read the letters without comment. He would reserve opinion on Major André until he had seen him. As for Benedict Arnold—what could anyone say of him, the most arrogant, shameless and villainous of men?

22

DARKNESS AND TENSION

ROBINSON'S HOUSE SEEMED THAT EVENING TO BE FILLED WITH officers. From many quarters they assembled, to counsel with the commander-in-chief; and except for the thud of their heavy boots, the rattle of spurs and clank of sabers, they were very quiet, their faces impassive.

Outside, in the barn, the enlisted men huddled for shelter from the driving rain; and they too were quiet, speaking only in low tones. Some of them knew what this day had meant, and might mean to the cause to which they had pledged their lives; others of them could guess; still others were merely bewildered and oppressed with the feeling of suspense.

When the officers sat down to the dinner which Catherine Martin and Emmeline had prepared, Colonel Varick presided at the head of the table. But he was not his amiable self tonight. The fever crimsoned his cheeks; he was awkward and distrait. He had no appetite. But then, the appetites of all the diners were dull, and the delicious food so plentifully supplied, was carried back, almost untasted, to the kitchen.

"Well, anyway," said Catherine, looking at the heaped platters, "it'll not go to waste. I'll parcel it out among those hungry lads out there. And I wager it'll be the best rations they've had in months—and a grand change from hardtack!"

"Catherine," Emmeline said, "you are fine. So thought

ful, and so sensible. You seem to know what to do in any emergency. I wish I could be like that!"

"It's all practice," said Catherine. But she was pleased, nonetheless, and some of the lines of sheer physical weariness smoothed out of her brow as she smiled.

"Since dawn you've been on your feet, never stopping a minute."

"And you have, too. But we mustn't be *dreaming* of stopping yet, Emmeline. We've oceans of work before us—and who can prophesy when Mistress Arnold may have another bout with the hysterics and we'll be fetching hot and cold water, and all the rest? Here, if you're going to dodge out for a word with your brother, take him this biscuit with jam on it."

Soon after the meal, which had been nearly completely silent, General Washington asked Colonel Varick to walk with him on the veranda. They went out and strode up and down. The rain made a curtain between them and the trees, and drilled on the roof above them. Intermittently there was the roll of distant thunder.

"Colonel, I now have indisputable proof of Arnold's perfidy."

"I feared as much, sir," said Varick, "and I am sorry for it." His face was strained and grief-stricken in the gleam of candlelight filtering from the windows.

"I have as yet no reason to believe that you or Major Franks were implicated."

"I assure you we were not, sir. No one could have been more surprised than we were—or more horrified."

"Arnold has written me that you are guiltless. But you will realize that what he says is worth less than nothing. The truth is not in such a man."

"I do realize that, sir; and so will Major Franks."

"It may seem strange to the public that you two were so

intimately associated with Arnold here, and yet did not know of his scheming. Were you never suspicious?"

"We thought," said Varick, "that he might be dishonestly dealing in the army's stores—indeed, I was positive of that, for I investigated and was convinced. We thought also that he was endangering his reputation by granting too many flags to people known to be Loyalists. We knew he was writing messages in code; and that he might be sending the messages to Philadelphia by a man called Hugg or by other hirelings. We knew of his correspondence with John Anderson and we did not like it. Most of all, we abhorred his friendship with that despicable Joshua Smith! But we never thought he would seek to betray his country!"

Messages in code, flags to Loyalists, the unscrupulous selling of provisions? "Why did you not speak of these things, Colonel Varick?"

"We should have, sir." Varick sighed. "Arnold always had some plausible excuse—which we accepted. And there was his military glory, his daring and gallantry in the past—"

"That blinded you?"

"It made us hesitate to accuse him where we would have been quick to accuse a lesser man." Varick paused, and then said: "And both Franks and I had been fond of him."

"He has many qualities of mind and manner to deceive the beholder. But at heart—"

"At heart he is a criminal! I see that now!" Varick shuddered. "Franks and I had planned to leave him. I believe that Franks asked for a transfer, and intended to ask again. I had resolved upon it, too, because of my certainty that he was smuggling stores into the cellar of this house; because of the Smiths; because of his communications with John Anderson. We were to tell him that we were leaving—before it should be too late. And now it is too late!"

"I am afraid so. Too late for you to avoid being besmirched with his dishonor."

They walked the length of the veranda, beneath the relentless tattoo of the rain.

"Colonel Varick," said Washington austerely, "my duty as an officer makes it necessary for me to inform you that you must regard yourself as my prisoner. You will be kept here under guard and will come to trial with Benedict Arnold, as soon as he shall be taken."

Varick bowed his head. "This is not unexpected, Your Excellency. But I will be acquitted of any complicity."

"I hope you will. I have faith that you will. In such a disaster many virtuous folk must suffer disgrace and pain—which in itself should be enough to deter a man from wrongdoing!" Washington reflected briefly. "The servants in the house? What do you know of them?"

"Besides the soldiers who have gone back and forth in relays from the fortress, there are but three. Mistress Arnold's maid, Bolton, and Catherine Martin; and the young girl, Emmeline Drake—her family lives in the vicinity, country people."

"Emmeline? I noticed her. She has not the appearance of a conspirator. Bolton we may rule out also; she would be as innocent as the lady she attends. But Catherine Martin must be questioned; she may have had guilty knowledge, especially as to the stores hidden in the house."

"But Catherine Martin has been employed by the Arnolds for several years, sir; her husband is a soldier—"

"I must remind you, Colonel Varick, that neither fact would clear her of suspicion . . . Come, let us go in where there is a fire."

At ten o'clock Catherine mixed a bowl of hot rum punch for the company in the library. The officers sat about, conversing in sober voices, waiting for the arrival of Major André who was on his way here through the stormy night.

Catherine dropped to a stool in the kitchen and leaned her head in her hands. She was yawning, but said she could not go to bed. A house abandoned by its master and neglected by a mistress who was ill must have someone to look after it.

"The guests might want me. I'll stick to my post," Catherine said.

Then her head slipped down upon the table and she dozed.

The hours were very long, as measured by the clock on the kitchen shelf, but Emmeline was wakeful. Her thoughts raced from one development of this disturbing day to the next. How strange everything was! Robinson's House, though so large, seemed much too small to hold all the woe which had befallen it. Tonight in each room were anxiety and disillusionment; upstairs, Mistress Arnold lying in a drugged stupor; Dr. Eustis solemnly watching his capricious patient; Bolton sniffling into her handkerchief while she hushed the colicky baby—downstairs, the officers, solicitous and stern; Major Franks so grim that the scar on his chin showed bone-white; Colonel Varick with tremulous hands and eyes too bright. In the yard sentinels patrolled, and in addition to these guards and the soldiers in the barn, a cordon of troops had been thrown all around the property, with sentinels strung in a line from Beverley Dock to the veranda.

And by the kitchen hearth, with a tallow candle and the ticking clock, Emmeline herself and poor, tired Catherine.

Yet for all that so many people clustered within the space of perhaps a mile square, Emmeline had never felt more lonely in her life; and she thought the others must be lonely, too. For they were people who had been robbed of their trust in a fellow human being, forced to see the depths to which a creature like themselves could sink.

"And that," Emmeline thought, "makes you lonely."

She recalled the day she had come to this place, her first impressions of it as gloomy and somehow frightening—and of all the days after, when the gloominess and the vague foreboding had increased. She knew now that she would have few more days here. Soon she'd be going home.

"I can't imagine how I've stayed all this while. I'll not stay now!"

She yearned for the sight of Granny and Kirby and the cottage. That would make everything right again!

But the idea of going home conjured up another thought, of something she must do, something she was determined to do, before she left, something which would comfort her.

The kitchen door creaked and a man was in the room, a captain, one of the younger officers who had dined with General Washington. Emmeline did not know his name.

"Are you Catherine Martin?"

"No. That's Catherine, sir." Emmeline pointed. "Please let me serve you, sir."

"I am to question Catherine Martin."

Emmeline's eyes widened. "You don't—surely no one could think that Catherine—"

"Was in the plot? If so, we'll find out."

"But Catherine is a patriot!"

"Suppose I said she was not?"

"It would be a—a falsehood!"

"Suppose I said she was a cunning Loyalist schemer?"

"No!" Emmeline said. "Oh, no! You *couldn't!*"

"Well, well!" The captain looked amused. "Catherine has a stanch defender."

"She doesn't need defenders, sir, for she has done nothing. I've been with her almost every minute of every hour for weeks and weeks—I know what she is. A true American! And so are Colonel Varick and Major Franks. They're gentlemen and patriots. They had no part in whatever General Arnold planned."

"You'd take an oath on that?"

"A thousand oaths! I would!"

"You'd swear to the integrity of this woman—and Varick and Franks? The three of them?"

"I'd swear it! And don't you think, sir, that you can tell whether people are good or bad? Maybe not so much by speech and deeds; it's more a feeling you have about them." She was earnest; never in all her fifteen years had she been so earnest. "Don't you think there *is* such a feeling, sir?"

"Instinct? Intuition?"

"It's just—*knowing*. I know that Catherine and Colonel Varick and Major Franks are good. I'd risk my life on them." She hesitated. "Will you say that to General Washington, sir? Say it to everybody. Say that I'm young—of course, I am!—but not too young to be able to know good people from bad."

The captain smiled rather curiously. "I will say that, if you wish me to."

"Oh, thank you, sir. And please don't wake Catherine!"

"We'll just let Catherine drowse a bit," said the captain.

It was four o'clock, five. Morning was dawning in the east when Major John André came to Robinson's House. The rain had thinned to a drizzle, but he was soaking wet from head to foot, and so were the soldiers who had brought him.

Emmeline saw Major André get down from his horse. The sodden coat he wore was the very one Granny had stitched for Mr. Joshua Smith! Whoever would have guessed that this was to be its fate? The claret silk clothing a spy!

But Major André in the library was contending something else.

"I am not a spy," he said to the men he faced. "I should not be made to pay the penalty for spying—and I am quite well aware what that penalty is!"

"You had these documents?"

"I had them. But I am not a spy." He repeated it with dogged persistence, over and over, in a calm, cold voice.

His accusers told Major André he would have to be court-martialled. He would be transported across the river at once to West Point, and then down to Tappan. He would be given a fair trial, according to law. Justice would be speedy.

He was promised that—and nothing more.

23

HOMEWARD-BOUND

EMMELINE OPENED HER EYES AND THOUGHT: "WHAT DAY IS this? What have I to do?"

Oh, yes! It was October second—and she was going home!

She was leaving Robinson's House; tonight she would be seeing Grandmother and Kirby; tomorrow morning she would waken in her own bed, in her own room in the cottage. The joy of that overshadowed everything else.

She did not immediately spring up. There was no hurry, no routine of tasks today. Before noon a skiff would come from West Point to Beverley Dock, a soldier would row her to Buttermilk Falls. Meanwhile she had few chores of any sort. Her clothes were packed; when she had dressed and made her bed, the little chamber under the eaves would be ready for its next occupant—whoever that might be. Probably the chamber would be tenantless a long time; Robinson's House was being closed now and nothing had been said of its reopening.

Emmeline thought of the week just past. It had been crowded, but its incidents had seemed like an anticlimax compared to the excitement of that day of General Washington's visit. This was like the final scene of a play—the main theme over and done with, and the remaining characters to be disposed of. One by one, these remaining characters were going their separate ways.

Mistress Arnold had been the first. After the interview

with General Washington, she had recovered from the hysterics and, miraculously, never had a recurrence. Not only did Washington grant her permission to travel to Philadelphia, but he said that Major Franks must escort her. On September twenty-seventh, scarce forty-eight hours after she had been in a condition of collapse, she was well enough to set out on the journey.

Emmeline had watched Mistress Arnold's exit from Robinson's House, and had reflected that it was quite similar to her entrance. Once again she had been borne tenderly down the path to the river and the waiting boat; once again soldiers surrounded her, with Major Franks marching in front. Of course, the lady's husband was absent on this occasion; but Colonel Varick and Colonel Alexander Hamilton were in attendance, to spare her any embarrassment or discomfort; and General Washington had admonished that she be shown consideration in proportion to her terrible bereavement.

Mistress Arnold had wept delicately as she was leaving. She had forgotten to say goodbye to Catherine or to Emmeline or any of the humble folk who had served her here; but she had smiled bravely through tears at Colonel Varick as he waved to her from the dock. Colonel Varick had then trudged back to the house and played melancholy tunes on his violin.

What Colonel Varick did not know (or Major Franks, or anybody, for that matter) was that the following day Mistress Arnold had made some rather startling admissions. Stopping at Paramus, at the home of Mistress Theodosia Prevost, who was her friend (and who was later to marry Aaron Burr) Mistress Arnold had said that she was thoroughly bored with the theatricals she had been exhibiting. She had corresponded, she said, with Sir Henry Clinton for months. She was disgusted with the American cause and those who had the management of public affairs; through her unceasing perseverance she had brought the General into an arrangement to surrender West Point. Unfortunate that the arrangement had not worked out according to schedule!—but it might have been so much more unfortunate, for she was being treated with gentleness and forbearance, and the General was quite safe aboard the British vessel.

With only Colonel Varick and Catherine and Emmeline in it, Robinson's House was very still. Catherine had cleaned it, scouring and polishing everything, but she labored more to keep busy than to produce an effect. Thus far, Catherine had not been accused as a plotter, though she had spoken sadly of the possibility of this. ("Me! It's so silly! What could *I* have done?") Since Benedict Arnold had not been captured, Colonel Varick was to be given a hearing in a court of inquiry at West Point sometime in the near future. At this court Major Franks would also testify.

Most grievous experience of all was that of Major John André. Gossip had wafted back the tale from Tappan, where the young British officer was locked up in Mabie's tavern, a huge stone building which had once been a mansion house. Joshua Smith was a fellow prisoner of André's in the tavern, but the two men spoke not one word to each other. Brought to trial, Joshua Smith had been acquitted of the charge of treason. He was merely a deluded and misguided person, the court decided, who had been used as a pawn by Benedict Arnold; a man of small wit who had believed that he was engaged in performing some trick of cunning by which the war could be ended—and with a victory for the Americans. When he was freed, Mr. Smith had gathered up his family and bustled them all off to New York City—which some people thought a strange move, indeed!

But Joshua Smith's doings were lost sight of in the greater sensation of Major John André's court-martial.

He had been tried at Tappan in the old Dutch church, which stood beside the post road. The church, with its whitewashed walls of brick and stone, its ancient steeple with the bronze bell and the flag-shaped weather-vane, was a landmark. Built in 1699, its pulpit and communion table were imported from Holland. Generations of worshippers had walked through the grove of locusts and elms, beside the brook and through the graveyard to this little house of God. And on Friday, September 29, 1780, Major John André came there to confront the board of generals who would judge him.

All this while the British had not known where André was being held—for this was one secret which the Americans had successfully guarded. Frantically, Sir Henry Clinton had attempted to find out the place of his imprisonment; and the British commander and Beverley Robinson and Benedict Arnold, from the refuge of the *Vulture,* were dashing off frenzied letters in his defense.

But he was alone, a solitary figure in a claret-colored silk coat, sizes too large for him, when he went before the military tribunal.

His story was just as it had been at the time of his arrest. He told of the long period of communication with Benedict Arnold—a year and a half that had gone on! Some of Arnold's letters were signed *Gustavus,* and others had various fantastic signatures. In the "mercantile language" which Arnold affected, a pound meant an American soldier. When Arnold wrote, "My partner has £10,000 cash in hand and ready for a speculation if any should offer which appears profitable," André had understood that the "partner" was Washington and his soldiers were ten thousand. The "speculation" was Arnold's delivery of the Highland fortresses to the British.

Or sometimes Arnold had resorted to a code of numbers, as in the letter informing Sir Henry Clinton and André of Washington's halting at Peekskill. How few troops were with His Excellency then! How easily he could have been overpowered—abducted! And that thought had been in Arnold's mind. At Peekskill he had expected some group of assailants to rush out from the forest every moment and seize Washington. He would have shammed resistance—and spurred on the assailants in every way possible.

But, for reasons never explained, the British did not take the hint.

André said that from the first he had understood Benedict Arnold; there had never been any doubt as to the identity of *Gustavus*. Sir Henry Clinton and André were dealing with a traitor, a desperate one, and they knew it. Nor had Arnold been in the dark about André, though he called him his merchant friend, John Anderson. Their correspondence could have but one object—West Point was to be betrayed to the British, a master stroke to give Clinton victory over the colonies. Sir Henry had coveted West Point. He had suggested that Benedict Arnold seek the command there. And Arnold had been eager to do so. No position in the field, nothing else than control of the Hudson fortifications could have been reconciled with the elaborate, unscrupulous plot he was weaving.

For a while, the space of hours, it had seemed that he wasn't to get the appointment. But then, at Tappan, General Washington had acceded to his plea.

Major André contrasted his lot with Arnold's. "I have desired only to serve my king—whereas Arnold acted only for personal gain." Fifty thousand dollars was Arnold's price; the British had agreed to it. Even now he fumed and chafed that the payment was delayed. He had done his part! If the plot had crashed, it was not because of his failure. Wasn't he still entitled to his fee?

"When will I be paid?" Arnold was asking. "How soon? I need money. I must have it! *Pay me!*"

And didn't this show the difference between the two principal conspirators? André argued that it did.

"What is my crime? Would not any soldier of any country, any American, so commissioned, have striven to obtain intelligence which would mean his country's triumph?"

Was Major André, in fact, a spy?

The trial turned upon that question, that technicality.

In his speech of defense, André said he had never wished to venture within the American lines, never intended to. That was Arnold's doings. The boat had come for him in the black night and he had not wanted to get in. Reluctantly, when Joshua Smith pressed him, he had consented to being rowed ashore, to the copse of fir trees at the foot of Long Clove Mountain. The whole procedure had seemed bizarre to him, the conference lasting until daylight. And then his discovery that he was not to be taken back to the *Vulture*— no, instead, he had gone to Smith's house, feeling that this was ill-starred, an error which might not be redeemed.

Even more reluctantly he had afterward consented to the disguise of the silk coat—

"This hateful coat, gentlemen, which I am now wearing!"

The court asked him closely whether he had acted under Arnold's orders.

"At all times, and against my will, contrary to my discretion. I felt such a course to be perilous."

"Major André, was a flag of truce displayed on the boat of the Cahoon brothers?"

"No, gentlemen. There was no flag. None of any kind."

They quizzed him especially on this detail, for Sir Henry Clinton, Beverley Robinson and Arnold all were saying just the opposite, that Major André did have a flag—which would have marked him as an emissary, an intermediary and not a spy.

He told the truth. "I had no flag. I relied upon Arnold for safe conduct."

"Where did you change your attire? Within our lines?"

"At Joshua Smith's house. Within the American lines."

"Disguised and under a feigned name, you passed the works at King's Ferry?"

"With Joshua Smith. Yes, gentlemen, I did."

"And you had then in your possession several documents and papers which contained intelligence for the enemy?"

"The papers procured from General Arnold. Yes, gentlemen, I had them then."

The judges retired, deliberated—and returned with their verdict.

Major André was a spy. The court had ruled that he was not an emissary, an intermediary coming out under instructions from his government, or with the knowledge of his superior office, to *arbitrate* with an enemy. Rather, his was a solitary expedition, without a flag, without Sir Henry Clinton's permission; thus unprotected, he had come into territory held by his foes.

He was, therefore, a spy.

According to the law and usage of nations, he must suffer death.

He heard the verdict coolly. He was condemned.

But still he hoped that something would intervene to stay execution of the sentence, an exception would be made. He hoped he would not have to die.

He did not want to die.

When Emmeline went downstairs, Catherine was washing Colonel Varick's breakfast dishes.

"What do you think, Emmeline! I am not to be examined, after all!"

"Oh, I'm glad!"

"Yes, it would have been a thing shameful to remember. And how would my husband have felt, and all my relatives? They wouldn't have wanted to claim me! But now I've nothing to worry about. Mr. Richard just told me. He had a message which said that I was blameless. Someone has spoken in my behalf, Emmeline, though I don't know who it could have been—unless it was Mr. Richard himself."

"Perhaps it was," said Emmeline, with a little smile. She went to the table and put down on it a twisted handkerchief. "Catherine, you will be here for a while longer, won't you?"

"Until Major Franks returns to get his luggage. A week, maybe two weeks." Catherine nodded. "Why?"

"My half-crowns are there." Emmeline gestured toward the handkerchief. "My wages. I want you to give them back to the Major."

"But what in creation!"

"I couldn't take the money, Catherine. It came out of Benedict Arnold's purse. How do I know but that it got into his purse by treachery? It isn't patriot's money—which is the only kind I would want."

"Now, Emmeline! You've earned it and you must keep it."

"No." Emmeline was firm. This was the thing she had resolved upon that night a week ago, when it seemed the very earth was crumbling. "No, I can't keep it. I won't."

"Then you've worked here all this time for *nothing*?"

"Oh, no! I've learned a great deal."

Catherine folded her hands beneath the crackling white apron. "But you were working for a certain purpose, not just as I do, for a livelihood, because it's what I was trained for."

"Yes, I was. It was for Granny, her birthday present. But I know Granny would feel quite the same. We couldn't take money we weren't sure of. Traitor's money. Will you give it back to Major Franks?"

"All right," said Catherine, after a pause. "I will." She shook her head until the bow in her hair quivered like a butterfly on the wing. "You're an odd girl, Emmeline—but a good one."

Colonel Varick himself carried Emmeline's bundle to Beverley Dock, and neither of them seemed to notice the guard who kept the Colonel always in sight. Colonel Varick did not talk much, but strode through the autumn sunshine, his tall head stooped, his eyes vacantly staring.

When the boat came up, he helped her in and clasped her hand.

"Thank you, Emmeline. And the best of luck!"

"I wish you luck, too, sir."

"And I believe I'll have it!" Suddenly he smiled down at her. "Yes, I feel that I'll be exonerated of these odious suspicions. Several people have put in a word for me—and my record is clear. I am not afraid."

The boat pushed off; and Emmeline said: "Goodbye, Colonel Varick."

Once, in midstream, she looked back and saw him, thin and sandy-haired, silhouetted against the gray-green of the willow trees.

The boat took Emmeline to Buttermilk Falls. From there she would walk down the road—and perhaps beg a ride in a farmcart. Surely someone she knew would be on the highway, some neighbor from the Donderberg settlement.

It was not such a home-going as she'd ever imagined.

Tomorrow was Granny's birthday, and Emmeline had not one cent for the fund which was to start Granny off to Uncle Tom's.

"I've failed," said Emmeline to herself.

But maybe Jed had been more fortunate. Or Kirby. She hoped so!

24

"A MOMENTARY PANG"

JED WAS AT TAPPAN THAT MORNING OF THE SECOND OF October, detailed as a sentry in the corridor of Mabie's tavern—and it was the last place in the world he would have chosen to be. As he trod the narrow passage, he turned his eyes away from a certain barred door. Behind that door was Major John André who, at noon, would be executed. To Jed Drake, this fact seemed incredibly harsh—though he told himself that both the trial and the sentence had been fair, and there could be no appeal.

"It's law," he thought, "and custom and war. André *is* a spy, whether or not by his own intent. Instead of weeping for him, I must remember what it would have meant if he had not been caught. The fall of West Point, perhaps the defeat of all our hopes! And all those other men who have been killed in all the battles—they would have given their lives in vain. I must remember that."

He thought bitterly of Benedict Arnold, who now was hale and hearty, safe and sound with Sir Henry Clinton in New York. Most likely, Arnold would go to Canada or to England, escaping any sort of punishment. There was injustice for you! Jed believed, with many Americans, that the British should have turned Arnold over to them in exchange for André, who then would have been freed.

Letters on this subject had shuttled back and forth, and even so influential a person as Alexander Hamilton had pled for the exchange. But Sir Henry Clinton had refused—and, of course, Benedict Arnold had been against it. He much preferred association with the British who, he said, understood him better. He was proclaiming himself a hero, and one not properly appreciated by his countrymen. He was sorry for Major André—oh, yes! "But *I* have no responsibility in the affair. People are insane to say that André is an honorable man sacrificed to the greed of a dishonorable man. *I* am not greedy."

But still he must remind Sir Henry Clinton that none of the fifty thousand dollars had yet been paid. "I need money, sir. I must have it!"

From a window at the corridor's end, Jed looked down upon the tavern lawn and a gathering crowd. Feeling ran high among civilians; all week they had beleaguered the prison, wanting a glimpse of André. The sentries had toiled to keep these visitors within limits; but this morning they were more than ever unruly. Talk buzzed among them of Nathan Hale, the American whom the British had executed four years ago.

"Twenty years old he was. Just a lad. And did the Britishers show Nathan Hale any mercy? No, they did not! Called him a spy, they did, and killed him! So why should they now be asking mercy for André? The Englishman's got to die, too. It's in the Bible, an eye for an eye, a tooth for a tooth—"

Mounted officers were arriving. By twelve o'clock most of the American generals and field officers would be here—though not the commander-in-chief. His Excellency, General Washington, was in temporary seclusion; men nearest him knew how very worried he was, how much he wished that some circumstance might come to light by which André might be reprieved.

But, alas, there was nothing. Nothing at all . . .

The prison sentries had talked among themselves of

Major André. Without exception they respected him; they would not relinquish the thought that even yet his life might be spared. They had learned a good deal about André—he was a native of London, the son of Swiss-born parents. As a boy he had been educated in Geneva, returning to England at the age of eighteen. He became then a clerk in a counting-house, work which never satisfied him, for his interest was in literature and the arts. He was really a poet and a painter—until 1775, when he had joined the army and sailed for America.

So courageous and talented was the young man that he soon won the affectionate regard of Sir Henry Clinton, and quickly rose to the rank of major. He was Sir Henry's close friend and his adjutant general; he was beloved by the British troops—as well as by King George himself.

André's guards at Tappan said that he was frank and courteous; his gentle demeanor under the most adverse conditions had impressed not only the court which judged him but all who saw him in his cell. Never once did his valiant spirit falter. As he awaited the court's verdict, knowing what it must be, with evidence so overwhelmingly against him, he had been writing a graceful letter to Sir Henry, absolving his chief from all blame in this catastrophe:

"I am perfectly tranquil in my mind and prepared for any fate to which an honest zeal for my King's service may have devoted me . . . With all the warmth of my heart I give you thanks for your Excellency's profuse kindness to me. And I send you the most earnest wishes for your welfare."

He had no complaints to make of his treatment in prison.

"I receive the greatest attention from his Excellency, General Washington, and from every person under whose charge I happen to be placed."

As was only natural, he had continued to hope for a

commutation of his sentence. Perhaps Benedict Arnold would yet come forward with some plausible solution of the problem—instead of peppering General Washington with all sorts of absurd threats of violent retaliation. Perhaps General Washington would liberate John André if the British would liberate large numbers of their American prisoners of war.

When he knew finally that this was not to be, that Arnold was in New York, that General Washington had pondered and affirmed the court's conclusion, André was still composed, even smiling.

So he must die?

The manner of his death had troubled him most. In a note to General Washington, he asked that he might be shot like a soldier rather than hanged on the gallows like a felon.

He was concerned, too, about his clothing which had grown so soiled, the tattered rags of a beggar. And Joshua Smith's coat—it was the badge of indignity!

The officials at Tappan had allowed his servant to come out to him with fresh, clean linen and the British uniform of which he was so proud. Flinging the claret-colored silk garment into a corner, he put on his beautifully tailored scarlet coat, his sashes, his splendid sword with the gold hilt—and looked a gentleman again.

As Jed turned, sighing, from the window, he heard the rattle of a door and saw Major André's servant emerging from the cell to the corridor. He carried a tray and, with his hands so encumbered, could not wipe away the tears which streaked his cheeks and wet the front of his modest livery. The servant paused, and said to Jed:

"My master is up; he has bathed, shaved and dressed, and breakfasted on food fetched to him, as all his meals have been, from the table of General Washington. He is writing letters to his sisters and to his mother in England. With pen and ink he has sketched a picture of himself, clad in regimentals, seated in there behind the bars. He was gratified when, earlier, one of your majors informed him that his watch has been bought back from the skinner, Paulding, and that the watch will be sent to his family across the ocean."

The servant's voice broke, but as if he must tell someone of his grief, he went on: "I am weeping now, but I did not weep when I was in that room. Yesterday I sobbed at my first sight of him. And do you know what he said? 'Leave me!' he exclaimed. 'Leave me, until you can show yourself more manly.' So this morning I did not let him see my tears . . . What time is it, please?"

"It's half after ten," said Jed.

"Then there is but one hour and thirty minutes—"

"That's all."

The servant shook his head and proceeded along the corridor.

At something after eleven o'clock, Jed saw General Lafayette on his horse cantering through the milling throng outside the tavern. He vaulted from the saddle. For an instant Jed's breath was fast in his throat. The Frenchman had been so ardently in favor of André's reprieve. Was it possible that he had good news?

But one look at Lafayette's mournful face told Jed that he had no news. There would be no news now.

At noon, Major André picked up his hat.

"I am ready, gentlemen, at any moment to wait on you."

"And we are ready, sir."

With a soldier's tread he marched out of Mabie's tavern, an American officer on either side of him. One of these Americans was Major Tallmadge, who had been the first to know that this extraordinary spy was the adjutant general to Clinton. Tallmadge had grown to admire his distinguished prisoner and could not now conceal his emotion. His countenance seemed blurred and mottled, his bosom heaved with stifled sobs. But John André was calm.

Only as he rounded the bend in the path and viewed the gallows did he flinch. Was he to hang? Had he been denied the dear request of a soldier's death?

"Sir," Major Tallmadge said, "why do you halt?"

"Forgive me. I am reconciled to my death—but I detest the mode! Ah, well, it will be but a momentary pang."

And he marched on.

From his pocket he took two white handkerchiefs and bandaged his own eyes.

"Sir," said Tallmadge, through tears, "if you desire to speak, you have the opportunity to do so now."

He lifted the handkerchiefs from his eyes.

"I pray you to bear witness that I meet my fate like a brave man."

The noose was sprung.

In utter silence the crowd watched; in utter silence the crowd slowly dispersed.

And Major Tallmadge muttered: "Thus died, in the bloom of life, the accomplished John André of the royal army, a gallant soldier and the friend of Sir Henry Clinton."

Jed did not know how he got back to his post in the corridor. He was dazed. He wished that he need not have seen this tragedy. He would never forget it.

He passed and repassed the empty room—and then he felt a hand on his shoulder.

"Drake?" It was the sergeant. "Why, lad, you're pale as a ghost! Are you sick?"

"No, no, sir. I'm all right."

"General Lafayette is asking for you. He has a courier's errand up around Stony Point. He said you were to go—and glance in at your family on the way."

"Oh, thank you," Jed said. *"Thank you!"*

Before the clock had struck again, Jed was off, rocketing up the road which led to home, the hill breezes fanning his hot forehead, the fresh autumn air filling his lungs, his heart gradually shedding its burden of woe.

He would see Grandmother. He would see Emmeline and Kirby and find out what they had done about Granny's birthday. Jed himself had done nothing; but perhaps the others had been more resourceful.

25

GRANNY'S SURPRISE

NOTHING COULD HAVE BEEN PLEASANTER, KIRBY WAS SURE, than their being together again, all the Drakes, in the kitchen of the cottage. There was a kind of magic in this scene, at the end of a wonderful day; it was like a dream come true—the supper dishes washed and put away and the brace of candles on the table, Granny in her chair, Emmeline bent over her knitting, Jed stretched out to rest on the floor—and Kirby himself simply bursting with the announcement he was just about to make.

What a lot Kirby had to say! He opened his mouth to say it.

But then Granny said something—a startling something. Benedict Arnold's terrible actions, she said, might shorten the war.

They all were amazed, and Kirby exclaimed: "You don't think *that!*"

"I do. We've been bickering and whining among ourselves. Now we'll forget our puny little quarrels and rivalries. This will knit us up into a strong people, unified—exactly as Emmeline is knitting up those separate strands of yarn into a solid fabric. That's what trouble does. It's pretty bad at the time, but in the long run it can have a good effect."

Jed raised himself on an elbow. "The Loyalists won't be threatening us so boldly—at least, not for a while. My sergeant told me that three days ago an effigy of Arnold was carted through the streets of Philadelphia and stoned by civilians. Probably many of them were the same civilians who used to fawn on him. I guess Philadelphians and other Loyalists know now that treason can be discovered and wiped out."

Emmeline glanced up. "Isn't it rather like a play? Benedict Arnold is the villain; and if Major André hadn't met Pauling and the other skinners, the play would have been a tragedy—and we might have a bullying British trooper in our house this minute."

Kirby felt impatiently that the conversation was digressing, but Emmeline's mention of a play interested him. "The skinners were the heroes, weren't they, Granny?"

"Heroes? Those rowdies?"

"But they *were* heroes!"

"Nothing of the kind! Rowdies," Granny repeated. "Roistering down that lane, hiding under bridges, ready to jump out and rob any traveler—and not concerned as to who their victim was."

"They captured André—"

"An accident. Purely an accident, Kirby. But now, I daresay, Paulding and his comrades will have their names carved up in granite. That's fame for you!"

Jed said: "If the skinners were so anxious to fight, they would have joined the army."

"Oh, they wouldn't like war," Granny said, "the drudgery and privation, the hunger and thirst—and wounds, perhaps death. Well, I don't like war, either. No decent person likes it. People ought to settle their differences in a civilized way, and maybe some day they'll have the sense to. Meanwhile we can be grateful for our patriots."

Emmeline smiled and clicked her needles. "Our patriots like Jed—"

"Oh, Emmy!" Jed murmured, and got red with embarrassment.

"I feel sorry about Major John André." Granny rocked and nodded. "Though what happened to him doesn't compare with Benedict Arnold's punishment."

"Arnold!" Kirby exclaimed. "How can you say that? Why, he went free!"

"He *seemed* to go free, Kirby—"

"He escaped!"

"I don't believe he did. He escaped with his life, but how about his reputation? No doubt he thinks he's very lucky, and he's finding a few friends to praise him."

"Not many," Jed said, "André despised him, and so do most of the British."

"And there's what history will say of him. A hundred years from now school children will learn that Benedict Arnold was a traitor. A black traitor!" Granny paused, and added, her voice very low and rather dreadful: "Black, black, *black!*"

"He might have lost the war for us," Jed said. "That's queer, isn't it? One man can lose a war for a whole nation —if he's in an important position and plots on the grand scale, as Benedict Arnold did. But one man couldn't *win* a war—"

"Because," Emmeline said, "winning is something else. It's *all* the people—thousands, or millions—all working and praying, everybody pulling in harness, straining, *trying*. Don't you think so, Granny?"

"Yes," Granny said, "and that's what we're going to have here."

A little silence fell. "Now," Kirby thought. "Now, I'll tell them."

But at that very instant footsteps shuffled outside in the dark, and somebody was loudly singing.

" 'Yankee Doodle came to town,
Riding on a pony,' " ...

"It's Molly!" Emmeline cried. "Captain Molly!"

Jed grinned. "Ask her in."

Emmeline hurried to the door, and soon Captain Molly Pitcher was standing on the threshold, her hat cocked pertly on her red hair, the military jacket buttoned to her chin.

"Good evening." Molly saluted smartly. "Good evening, all."

"Won't you have a cup of tea with us, Captain Molly?"

"Thank 'ee, Emmeline, I can't stop. Not tonight. I must be off to Buttermilk Falls, for I've much to do there. I'm moving, as I s'pose your Granny will have told you."

"Moving? Where?"

Molly laughed. "Ah, you'll know. You'll know." She winked broadly at Grandmother. "This muslin wall you have, Mistress Drake—nice for summer, but you must patch it up before the cold season, eh?"

"Yes," Granny said gravely, and then she laughed a bit too.

With a flourish of her hand, Molly turned and went out, and the Drakes could hear her again, in the road, singing robustly, at the top of her lungs:

" 'Father and I went down to camp,
Along with Captain Good'in,
Where we see the men and boys
As thick as hasty-*puddin'* ...' "

"Well!" Emmeline said. "What was she hinting at?"

Granny smiled. "Oh, Molly must have her little joke."

"But *you* laughed—"

"Did I?" Granny drew Kirby to her chair and patted his head. "Kirby, you haven't said much tonight. Is there nothing for you to tell us?"

GRANNY'S SURPRISE

Nothing! Kirby gasped, and then drew a deep, deep breath. This was his moment.

"Listen," he shouted. "Listen, everybody! *I have sold my pigs!*"

He stared around at them and was satisfied with what he saw. They were dumbfounded.

"You?" Jed cried.

"Sold—" Emmeline began.

"Your pigs!" exclaimed Grandmother.

"It was today," he said, when the suspense had grown unbearable. "I was out all day, walking and walking—everywhere. To Stony Point, to Haverstraw, to the Cahoons at Mr. Joshua Smith's place. Do you know the Cahoons, Jed?"

"No, I don't. Who are they?"

"Business people. That's how I know them. Through business. They're fine fellows if you understand how to get along with them. They're men who won't be hurried; they're big and burly—and they mutter. And finally, this afternoon, suddenly, they decided they would buy my pigs. You could have knocked me down with a feather! I said, 'Right now?' And Mr. Samuel Cahoon said, 'I'll buy your pigs right now.' And so he did!"

"And a very good thing, too," Grandmother commented. "Those pigs have gotten to be a nuisance. But what will you do with the money, Kirby?"

What, indeed! He had to chuckle at that. He reached into his pocket and extracted five silver half-crowns. He reached over and put the coins into Granny's lap, letting them slip, one by one, slowly, through his fingers.

"For you."

"Me?"

"For tomorrow. Your birthday."

"But, Kirby—"

"To take you to Uncle Tom's."

She was thoroughly bewildered. "Uncle Tom's? I—Won't you explain?"

"I'll explain," Jed said.

Then Jed told Grandmother all about that solemn, sacred pact, sworn by the light of the July moon, and of how they all had vowed to rescue her from danger and hardships. But of the three, only Kirby had been able to succeed, for Jed hadn't yet collected any of the pay due him, and Emmeline had refused the wages of Benedict Arnold.

"I'm thankful you did," Grandmother said. "Yes, yes, it's what you should have done, Emmeline. And isn't Kirby a splendid businessman? I'm proud of him!" She paused. "So you want me to go to Rhode Island, do you?"

They said in an eager chorus, "You must!"

She was silent a long time. Then she took off her spectacles and polished the lenses, which seemed to have mist on them. "You are the dearest children, all of you. And I—I am nothing but a stubborn old woman!"

"You mean you won't go?" cried Kirby, alarmed.

"That's just it. I won't." She pulled Kirby into her lap, with the silver half-crowns. "I'm a stubborn old woman, my roots are here, and here I'll stay. Because I know you can't run away from hardships; you have to live with them, face them, overcome them. For that matter, everybody has hardships to endure in such a period as this, and mine are too slight to mention. I'll never complain, for I have you three dear children to love me. We must be together as often as we can. I'd feel like a coward, going off to safety and leaving you behind!"

"Emmy could go with you. And Jed's in the army. And I'll be a hermit—"

"A hermit, Kirby?"

"I think it would be fun."

"But I have a secret of my own." Grandmother's smile was unsteady. "A secret and a surprise."

"What?" Kirby demanded. *"What?"*

"The house does need mending before winter sets in. I suggest we buy the material for the repairs with some of your half-crowns, and do the job ourselves."

"Jed won't be at home—"

"No, Kirby. We must manage without Jed. But you and Emmeline and I will do it. And Captain Molly."

"Captain—"

Granny laughed. "That's my surprise. Captain Molly Pitcher is moving in to spend the winter months with us."

"Oh," Emmeline said, remembering, "Molly has been so dissatisfied at Buttermilk Falls."

"She asked me to keep her here. I'm to sew her a dozen ruffled petticoats, and she'll be a member of the family. Molly isn't afraid of work, she can do a great many things— she says she can even build a stout wall and chimney. You see, it's a sort of trade. And how well it's turning out! Before the snow flies, we'll be snug and cozy as bears in a den—Emmeline, Kirby, Captain Molly Pitcher and I— with Jed dropping in whenever he possibly can for a few precious hours at home. I do declare this is the best birthday I ever had!"

Jed and Emmeline looked at Granny's shining eyes, and then at each other, and then at Kirby.

And Kirby looked dubious.

"Can I mix the plaster? Myself?"

"If you want to."

"And lay the bricks and stone? *Myself?*"

"Yes, Kirby."

"No, I can't. I haven't any trowel. I haven't any *tools.*"

"A kit of tools must be our first purchase with your money. You will supervise and tell the rest of us what to do."

"Why," Kirby said, "I believe it will be more fun than being a hermit *or* raising pigs!"

"We'll enjoy Captain Molly's company," Emmeline said.

"And if we should need you, Granny," Jed said, "you'll be here and not in Rhode Island." He grinned. "We always do seem to need you—don't we?"

"Certainly you do," Granny said briskly. "And I need you. That's how it is, with families." She got up and lighted her bedtime candle and went to the window. She pushed aside the curtain.

"My dears," she said, over her shoulder, "this is a beautiful country. Nowhere else in the world, I think, is the sky so blue by day, so wide and starry at night. No other hills and grass are so green, no trees so rich with fruit and foliage. America, my dears." Her voice was husky, but distinct. "There's not a king can conquer it. No king will ever live to conquer it, no emperor, or thief, or bandit, or invading army. This country belongs to God—and He will take care of it."